Fanny Frewen was born in 1924. At seventeen she ran away from home to become a Gunner on an Anti-Aircraft Site. After the war she went to Drama School and then worked on *Vanity Fair* and *Harper's Bazaar* before making her career in advertising where she wrote, among others, the first eighteen Oxo commercials. She now lives in Kent with her husband, Stephen, and writes full time.

G000045476

## ALSO BY FANNY FREWEN

The Tortoise Shell
The Sunlight on the Garden

# A Woman's Judgement

## Fanny Frewen

ARROW

Published by Arrow Books in 1998

1 3 5 7 9 10 8 6 4 2

Copyright © Fanny Frewen 1998

Fanny Frewen has asserted her right under the Copyright,
Designs and Patents Act, 1988, to be identified as the author
of this work

This novel is a work of fiction. Names and characters are the
product of the author's imagination and any resemblance to
actual persons, living or dead, is entirely coincidental

This book is sold subject to the condition that it shall not,
by way of trade or otherwise, be lent, resold, hired out, or
otherwise circulated without the publisher's prior consent in
any form of binding or cover other than that in which it is
published and without a similar condition including this
condition being imposed on the subsequent purchaser

First published in 1998 in the United Kingdom
by Century

Arrow Books Limited
20 Vauxhall Bridge Road, London SW1V 2SA

Random House Australia (Pty) Limited
20 Alfred Street, Milsons Point, Sydney,
New South Wales 2061, Australia

Random House New Zealand Limited
18 Poland Road, Glenfield
Auckland 10, New Zealand

Random House South Africa (Pty) Limited
Endulini, 5a Jubilee Road, Parktown 2193, South Africa

Random House UK Limited Reg. No. 954009

A CIP catalogue record for this book
is available from the British Library

Papers used by Random House UK Limited
are natural, recyclable products made from wood grown in
sustainable forests. The manufacturing processes conform to
the environmental regulations of the country of origin

ISBN 0 09 964971 3

Typeset by SX Composing DTP, Rayleigh, Essex
Printed and bound in Great Britain by
Cox & Wyman Ltd, Reading, Berkshire

To Mary,

for there is no friend like a sister

# I

'Court Number One. Chairman, Mr Trevor Bacon. Magistrates, Mr Charles Turner, Mrs Laura Fenby.'

Laura's legs trembled as she walked out of the door of the retiring room. The chairman ushered her through first. While accepting his good manners, she nevertheless stood aside to allow him to lead the way to the bench.

This was the first time Laura had sat on the bench. So far, during her training period, she had only been able to watch from the back of the court.

The chairman's chair was almost like a throne, the more so by being surmounted by the lion and the unicorn: '*Dieu et mon droit*'. Its back stood a foot higher than that of the chair in which Laura, her legs now buckling, was glad to sit. All she could think of was that this was rather like having a baby. You did something that caused it, then time passed with it almost forgotten, until suddenly something terrifying was happening that you couldn't get out of.

To her horror, she found that the first case had come and gone without her hearing a word of it. She was vaguely aware of the culprit in the dock, a wavering figure behind glass. The defending solicitor's delivery convinced Laura that she had added deafness to idiocy. Later, she would learn that defending solicitors in such cases were usually rushed in at the last moment, so no wonder their heads were bent downwards in a rapid attempt to make sense of the notes.

Seeking agreement that a case was suitable for summary trial, Mr Bacon turned to each of his colleagues. Laura nodded, and only hoped she would have agreed had she had the slightest idea of what it was all about. I am, she told herself, a magistrate, a JP, sitting on the bench. As each solicitor entered or left the court he or she bowed, with varying degrees of respect. Some of the older male solicitors bowed as formally as though they were facing a High Court Judge. One of the young women, who had been asked by the chairman please to speak up, contented herself with a tetchy bob. Her client had not got off.

Laura's first official day in court turned out to be a long one. A big case list entailed reconvening after lunch. She had planned to do some shopping for dinner then, but the court was far too far away from the shops to get there and back within the hour. Like the local crematorium, it occupied a pleasant and leafy site outside the town. Everyone but herself seemed to have matters of importance to discuss with one another during the lunch break.

She was not hungry. Being uncertain where she should go, she wandered out into the reception area. She had passed through it on her way in, some hours ago. It had seemed a pleasant place, shiningly clean, with comfortable seats and an abundance of the sort of standing ashtrays she associated with archaic gentlemen's clubs. In fact she had thought it kind, in this hysterically anti-smoking age, to see consideration given to the need for a nerve-soothing cigarette for people in trouble.

It seemed they could have saved on the ashtrays. Though the air was a Hiroshima of smoke, the ashtrays were redundant. But not the floor. Cigarette ends were piled like deep litter in a hen-house; polystyrene cups and tin cans, tissues and crumpled copies of the *Sun* completed the ghastly gala. This was in bizarre contrast to the human company. Their outfits, though perhaps not entirely respectful to the court, were almost all peacock smart, with the shining cleanliness of the brand-new. Her main impression was that, while many of the young men were overweight, their female companions were stick-thin, and made up as though for a television appearance.

When, at last, the court rose at the end of the day, Laura's attempt to go a modest last through the retiring-room door was foiled by the mannerly chairman, who held it open for her.

'Have you,' he enquired, 'found it interesting?'

'Very much so, thank you. Particularly since I had already seen that man who had been keeping drugs in his bathroom.'

'Where did you see him?' asked Mr Bacon.

'He was in the reception area. I went through there at lunchtime.'

'That's perhaps not a very good idea. We are not here to draw foregone conclusions. And it's as well not to mingle.'

On the way home, too late for the supermarkets, Laura managed to buy a limp lettuce at a wayside farm shop.

3

'I'm sorry, darling, dinner's a bit makeshift tonight,' she said to John as she got quiche out of the freezer and put it in the oven, where it burnt. Perhaps she ought to get a microwave.

'Perhaps I'd better learn to cook,' said John.

'I'm sorry,' Laura repeated. 'I didn't know it would go on all afternoon. But I think that's unusual.' She had been away a lot during the six-month training period which they described as an induction course. But she had prepared for that by doing big batches of cooking for the freezer, and remembering to take out what was needed in the morning before departing, so that meals, although inclining to casseroles and spaghetti bolognese, were on time.

Also, the training period had given John a benevolent sense of authority. As a solicitor, he was in a position to teach her quite a lot. Her virginity as a trainee magistrate was almost as pleasing as her virginity as a girl had been, all that long time ago. 'Magistrates' courts are usually through by lunchtime,' he now said. 'But never mind,' he added kindly, 'chuck this mess in the bin and I'll take you out to dinner.'

A few glasses of wine into the meal they were eating in one of the two high street restaurants, he was able to tell Laura how proud he was of her achievement.

'Lucky this place is a walking distance from home,' said Laura. 'Eminent solicitor and magistrate breathalysed! That would be a nice one for the local paper.'

Later on, in bed, John chuckled. 'We had a chap in court the other day who was giving a lot of lip. He was told to behave himself in front of the magistrate.'

'And did he?' asked Laura.

'No. He said, "Fuck the magistrate."'

4

## 2

A t times, during her training to become a magistrate, Laura had found herself saying, 'Whose
barmy idea was this?' and having to remember that it
was John's barmy idea, brought on by her own barmy
idea of trying to get a job.

'I wish,' she had said, 'I could write a novel. I
would, if I could write. If only I could do something
useful.'

'You've done a great deal that is useful,' said John.

'But I mean now.'

This conversation took place on the day that their
younger daughter, Ann, plus baby John Luke, were
collected from the Fenbys' home, the Grange, by her
husband, Len. At two years old John Luke was a sturdy
feeder, which was hardly surprising as his mother and
father were both chefs. So much so that he would yell
for sustenance in the middle of the night, a habit that
did not go down well with his grandfather.

'You've been marvellous, Mum,' said Len. 'We
would have been sunk without you. But we really can
manage now. You've done more than enough. And,
let's face it, a toddler is what you really don't need
around the house.'

True enough. But Laura woke up in the middle of

5

five nights in a row waiting for John Luke's roar and hearing only silence.

When she brought the subject up again with her husband, John said, 'The only sort of paid job you could get, my darling, would muck up my income tax for no good purpose.'

This was proved by the sort of job she was offered, if any. She learnt the hard way that bringing up four children and looking after an ageing and impossible mother are not qualifications in the job market. What she *was* offered was telephone selling, at which she was so lamentable that she fired herself after the first week, having spent a small fortune on petrol and parking fines and earned practically nothing.

Then she had the idea of taking a computer course, with a view to becoming a secretary. She quite liked playing with computers but decided, the first time she went for an interview and encountered a receptionist aged about eighteen, looking like a page three girl with clothes on, that she was too old for that lark. And John was right: what she might earn would make no difference to their already reasonably comfortable income, except in nuisance terms.

It was after the receptionist débâcle that he suggested she apply to become a magistrate, and she sent off the letter.

In the meantime there had been her elder son, Peter's, divorce. She was not particularly sad that he had split up with his wife. Laura had done her level best to become fond of Deirdre, so it came pretty much as a relief to be able to give up trying and admit to herself that she had never liked her, and never shared any common ground with her.

She thought fondly of her younger son, Luke, now uncle to John Luke, known as J. L. Darling. Luke in his early years had no intention of breaking hearts. He just took pretty girls to bed in a friendly manner, and was horrified and tender about the tears they shed when he finally put on his trousers for the last time and said goodbye. He would dry their eyes and say, consolingly, 'It wouldn't work, you know. I'm not good enough for you. You need a decent chap, and I'm not it. I'm just not husband material.'

He had now met his match, however, in the shape of his present mistress, Mary. Laura initially had been cross with Mary for leading him a dance. But even she, a doting mother, recognised that this was not fair. Mary, divorced and two or three years older than Luke, was as honest as a blade. She had said, both to him and to Laura, 'It would take a lot to get me to marry again. And I mean a lot, a lot of money. Darling Luke's idea of toil is to get a job for the shortest possible time to earn enough when he wants to buy another car.'

Laura wished Judy was as happy as Ann. Judy was almost a year older than Ann but, with Ann not only married but also a mother, she felt much older than that, an ageing bachelor girl possibly condemned to the single life for ever.

'But, darling,' said Laura, 'you're only just over thirty. And these days women with careers like yours often don't want to get married until they are in their thirties. Why rush? Look at how much you've achieved.'

Judy had, indeed, achieved. She was a successful executive, good-looking and also stunningly chic and well-groomed. Laura, having married young and rapidly become a mother, told herself that she envied Judy's freedom, earning power and choice of admirers. It saddened her to think that Judy might be in danger of tying up with a Mr Wrong simply on account of the damned biological clock.

That her venomous old mother, Veronica, regarded Ann as a kitchen maid who had married a potboy merely made Laura laugh. Ann and Len loved their baby, they loved each other, and they had enough lovingness in them to love her as well.

Some time after Laura had sent off the letter, and the edge of excitement about her new venture was blunted, little J. L., who was paying Granny a visit, was sitting on her lap undoing her buttons when the telephone rang.

'Mrs Fenby, about your application to become a magistrate – you will have received a letter.'

In fact J. L., who enjoyed his visits to Granny, had helpfully dealt with one morning's post by bringing Laura the pretty pictures. Doggies on the animal charity requests, pretty ladies in swimsuits on the catalogues, and a boring one with no pictures, which he tore up.

'As you know from the letter, we like to do the first interview in the applicant's home.'

Laura was sufficiently quick-witted not to ask what it was she was supposed to have applied for. And memory came back. 'Of course. When would you like to come?' she asked, mentally planning to get Mrs Bean, her cleaner, in for extra days in time to have the house looking respectable.

'Tomorrow. Would five o'clock be convenient?'

8

Although this was framed as a question, the voice announced it as a decision.

It was nearer six than five when Laura's interlocutors arrived at the house. There were two of them, a man and a woman. They looked tired, she thought. They must have had a long day. She could hear Mrs Bean upstairs, singing to J. L. as she bathed him, an act over and above the call of duty.

Naturally hospitable, she said, 'May I get you something? Sherry? A glass of wine?' This was not at all the right suggestion. 'Oh, of course, you are driving,' she said hastily, and offered coffee or tea. Both refused.

Serious business began. 'What makes you think you would be a good magistrate?'

'I'm not sure I would be. It was more my husband's idea than mine. I would never have thought of it myself.'

'Have you done much voluntary work?'

'None, I'm afraid. They asked me to be Brown Owl once, but I was having my fourth baby at the time and I couldn't have got into the uniform.'

'Your children – have they done well?'

'Yes and no. My elder son is living abroad. He is divorced, I'm afraid. My elder daughter is a business-woman, a successful one. My younger daughter is a chef, and she's married to a chef. They have a baby son. My younger son is . . .' She stopped, finding Luke's activities hard to define.

'You have a beautiful home.'

'Rather untidy, I'm afraid.' She had tidied but she had missed J. L.'s bunny, and it was now too late to kick it under the sofa. She leaned down and picked it up.

'Why,' they asked again, 'do you want to become a magistrate? Do you regard it as social advancement?'

'Certainly not,' said Laura and added, 'It must be very exacting work. Are you sure I can't get you at least a cup of tea?' Surely a cup of tea could not be construed as bribery? Right now what she most wanted was for them to go away, and never again to hear a word about being a magistrate.

It wasn't until the formal panel interview that she realised, expecting to be turned down, that that would disappoint her.

She had left the interview convinced that she could now put the whole thing out of her mind. After thirty-five years of listening to her children – 'Mummy, it's not fair.' '*Everybody* has tights.' '*Everybody* stays out till ten o'clock' – she found it quite extraordinary to be asked questions about herself and her views.

When asked what she felt about the police, the only policeman she could think of was Tom, the Swanmere bobby, who played a good game of cricket and, being a lazy fellow, spent a lot of time standing about in the High Street being friendly.

'The only one I know is an excellent peace-keeper,' she said. 'But it must be much more difficult in other areas.'

'So you think they do a good job?'

'Oh, yes indeed.'

Her voice proclaimed a good education and her husband was a prominent local solicitor. As his wife she was imbued with respect for the law, and she had raised four children. Little did she know that she was, in fact, the ideal magistrate, a trained listener.

# 3

As a rule, nothing of any moment took place in Swanmere without everybody knowing of it, frequently before it happened. The village owed much of its charm to its toy-town geography. The houses surrounding the green had arrived slowly, in a slower age, and as required by owners who knew nothing of architecture. Many of them propped each other up, shoulder to shoulder like friendly drunks. Supermarkets were a drive away and, although most prudent Swanmerians did their main marketing in them, some, particularly the oldest and gossipiest, still supported the High Street greengrocer, butcher and a shop that sold brides' mothers' hats, and silk dresses with matching coats, mostly beige.

Putative grannies discussed the pregnancies of their daughters and daughters-in-law. Actually, these days, the prognostications began when the young wives came off the pill. Laura once said with a sigh, 'Pregnancy seems to last eleven months nowadays.'

There was, however, one piece of news that did not get round, which was that Laura Fenby was going through the training procedure to become a magistrate. This was because she mentioned it to no one and swore her husband to equal secrecy.

It was during her first two training sessions that she realised how much greater a responsibility she was being prepared for than she had previously understood. Her own late father had been a magistrate. On the whole a merciful man, he made his decisions on the basis of the feller's face, being convinced (quite often correctly) that he knew by physiognomy who was a liar, who was a thief, and who was a poor dupe who had been set up by 'bad company'.

Sitting one day at the back of the court, Laura wondered what Daddy would have made of today's defendants. For a start, she was pretty certain that, except for the occasional prostitute in to pay her dues, he had seldom, if ever, seen a woman in the dock.

A dreary procession of drabs, charged with DSS fraud, made glib promises which they patently had no intention of keeping, to pay off their fines at the rate of five pounds a fortnight. In several cases their solicitors pleaded for leniency, on the grounds that having to support their drug habit wasn't their fault. And GBH, she learnt, was no longer a male preserve.

One particular defendant had managed to contrive a costume that gave her the appearance of a schoolgirl. She also had freshly washed hair. It was hard to believe that she had, with a broken bottle, taken out the eye of a girl who had been foolish enough to pinch the affections of her boyfriend. The disputed young man was in court, and Laura reflected sorrowfully that he didn't look worth the bother, never mind the custodial sentence coming the way of his previous mistress.

Watching the magistrates, Laura was filled with awe. Could she ever manage what they were managing? They listened. They watched. By the end of a long morning, she was finding it difficult to concentrate fully. Their attention never wavered. While far from unsympathetic, they were not deceived by plausibility.

Although she said to John, on more than one occasion, 'I'm never going to be able to do this,' some dogged streak she had never known existed made her persevere. Even so, she still kept absolutely quiet about what she was doing.

This earned her the nearest thing to a rebuke Dorothy Carew was capable of. Dorothy was the vicar's wife. She was some years older than Laura, and of the old school of vicars' wives. Over the years she had come to rely on Laura as her own curate. For Laura was a kind woman. When her own children were small, her attitude to having other people's children dumped on her was one of, 'Why not? I've got to give mine their lunch anyway, so one more makes no difference.' When newcomers arrived in the village, they were sure of a welcome from Mrs Fenby.

Thus it was that when Swanmere Cottage, opposite, was sold to Kenneth and Pamela Bartlett, Laura had accompanied Dorothy Carew on her first visit. 'We heard a lot about you from the Clarks, when they sold the house to us,' said Pamela.

'Oh yes?' said Laura. 'They were good friends of ours.'

'They went to America, didn't they? His job.'

'Yes. I'll miss them. But I do hope you'll be happy here.'

'I'm sure we will. She had very good taste, and we're so lucky that she left some furniture and all her curtains and carpets – a lot of them were brand-new.'

Pamela and Kenneth had a baby the same age as

Ann's J. L., and planned on having more. 'This is a perfect place for children,' she said.

'Mine loved coming here. They liked to play in the wild garden. You know, down at the bottom.'

'Oh, that. The waste space. We're going to clear that, and have a swimming pool built. With a fence round it, of course, for safety with little children.'

Pamela, who was a planner, had postponed the arrival of her first child until she was thirty-two, by which time Kenneth could afford a nanny. Now she decided to get on with the next one, and became pregnant again with efficient speed. But it was on the day before Laura's third training session that the nanny quit, just at the point when Pamela was being sick.

Dorothy Carew telephoned Laura. 'Laura, dear, can you help? Poor Pamela. I've promised her I'd ask you to take the toddler off her hands for a day.'

'I'm so sorry, Dorothy, but I can't. I won't be here.'

'What's the trouble? Is something wrong with your mother?'

There was nothing in the world wrong with Veronica Chadwick, now safely ensconced in Cathay Manor, an establishment for the well-to-do elderly which she, although a resident, ran with a rod of iron. 'No, Mother's perfectly all right.'

'What is it, then? Something wrong with Ann?' Dorothy could only envisage Laura in the capacity of waiting on members of the family.

'No.' Cornered, Laura came up lamely with, 'No, I just felt the need of a day to myself. To go shopping, and perhaps have lunch out.'

'But, dear Laura, surely you can do that any time? And Pamela really does need help with the little boy.'

Laura said, trying not to snap, 'I'm too old for toddlers. I don't know what to do with them any more.'

This, in Dorothy's book, was patent nonsense. Laura adored, and was wonderful with, Ann's little boy.

'I'm sorry, Dorothy, but I can't do it.'

'Are you ill?' Perhaps, thought Dorothy, Laura was going to see a specialist and with her usual thoughtfulness didn't want to worry anybody.

'No. I'm perfectly well. But there's something else I am doing, so I shan't be here. They've got plenty of money. Pamela can ring one of the agencies and get a temporary, or she could give employment to someone in the village.'

'Don't you like Pamela, Laura? This is so unlike you.'

'Of course I don't dislike Pamela. I hardly know her.'

'I can't think,' said Dorothy Carew to her husband, Theodore, 'what has come over Laura. I hope nothing is wrong between her and John. I asked her to help Pamela Bartlett, and all she would say was that she wouldn't be here, she had something else to do.'

'Perhaps,' said Theo facetiously, 'she's got a secret lover.'

It was equally difficult to get peace and quiet in which to study. Laura now paid the price for having always been the woman who didn't mind being dropped in on. Not only was Laura Fenby's house the place everyone went to for coffee and a moan, but there was also dear Mrs Bean.

The problem with Mrs Bean was that Laura was almost fonder of her than anyone else in Swanmere. It was many years since Mrs Bean had first taken on the job of cleaning for Mrs Fenby. Each successive child had loved her. And, although they had remained 'Mrs' to one another throughout, Laura Fenby and Agnes Bean had developed the trust that occurs between true friends. Not only was coffee together a ritual, but also Mrs Bean, after her work was done, usually spent another half-hour, normally relished by Laura, chatting.

There was no question of brushing Mrs Bean off now, and she came twice a week. So Laura was forced to study at night. John, over the years, had become accustomed to drifting off to sleep with the comforting feel of some part of his wife's anatomy to hand. Laura, now, waited until he was asleep, tiptoed out of bed without putting the light on, and tried to get downstairs without knocking anything over.

'I hate sleeping without you. It's so lonely,' John would complain.

'It's the only way I can study. I'm sorry, but it's very difficult to get time to myself during the day. It's hard enough getting to the training sessions without letting anybody know what I'm doing.'

'Why are you so adamant about that? People would be interested.'

'Too interested. And then what a fool I'd look if I didn't succeed.'

'Now that really is silly. You've already been accepted. You won't be dropped now unless you get drunk and kill someone in the car.'

'I don't intend to do that, but sometimes I can't help thinking they've made a great mistake. Honestly, darling, if I really feel I can't do it, surely it's better to resign sooner rather than later?'

'But you won't, will you?'

'No. I guess I won't.'

# 4

Although she was so universally kind and friendly that no one knew it, Laura did have favourites in Swanmere. Apart from dear Mrs Bean, there was Mrs Fortescue.

Mrs Fortescue was the widow of a commander in the navy. Commander Fortescue had been, during his lifetime, a selfish but extremely attractive man. Mrs Fortescue, adoring him, had sublimated her life entirely to his.

On his death, Quentin had left her with all his worldly goods: a somewhat eroded pension and a tiny, pretty house overlooking Swanmere's village green, with a lethal staircase under which was the cupboard which had served as his cellar. This was a veritable Pooh's honeypot cupboard, filled from wall to wall with bottles. They were stacked carefully on shelves beneath which stood case upon case of gin. It was this gin in which Mrs Fortescue now regularly sank her grief at her husband's death.

Laura was aware that Mrs Fortescue was a bit of a tippler. But many years of performing as a considerate hostess now stood the old lady in good stead. She was always gracious and courteous, even though sometimes the day ended with a bit of a struggle to get up the groggy staircase to bed.

She did not know that she was to join her late husband sooner than expected.

Mrs Fortescue had a friend who lived a few miles away from Swanmere. This lady, who was much happier to be a widow than was Mrs Fortescue, had telephoned in tears after having to have her dear old dog put down. Mrs Fortescue popped a bottle of gin on the back seat of her car, and set out on an errand of mercy.

On the way home, a car which was being driven too fast hit her head-on. It was occupied by a particularly nasty couple, who instantly called the police on their mobile telephone. The wife had a broken fingernail, an injury for which she demanded to be taken to hospital. Mrs Fortescue spent the night in a cell.

John Fenby, as her solicitor, defended her in court. He did the best he could, but could not protect her against having her age, which was eighty-two, read out aloud. She was three or four years older than Quentin but had managed to keep this a secret between herself and her birth certificate. Quentin had fortunately been merry enough on his wedding day not to notice the date of birth on the marriage lines.

This exposure might just as well have been a public stripping and whipping at the cart's tail. Mrs Fortescue was banned from driving for two years. But her death sentence had already been handed down. In three months, she was dead. Laura, who had a key to her house, found her at the foot of the stairs, already cold.

This tragedy took place during Laura's magisterial training period and rocked her confidence in her new vocation.

'John,' she said, 'that case killed her. How could they do that to her?'

'The law's the law. She was driving way over the limit. She could have killed someone.'

'But she didn't. Couldn't the police have turned a blind eye?'

'Certainly not. And if you think that way, then you shouldn't consider being a magistrate.'

'Maybe I shouldn't. I must say, if I'd been on the bench, I couldn't have sat and watched her being torn to pieces like that.'

'You wouldn't have had to. There's perfectly good provision for that. You sit back.'

Laura hadn't yet heard of that. John now explained. 'If a defendant is known to a magistrate on the bench, it is the rule that he or she sits back, and is detached from the case.'

'I'd have had to leave the court altogether.' However, much to her own surprise, the next day Laura gathered her courage and enthusiasm, pressed her skirt and jacket, and set off for her fourth training session.

Mrs Bean usually came on Mondays and Fridays. One Friday, Laura had to announce that the coming Monday would have to be a key-under-the-mat day. 'I won't be here. I'm doing a course of training.'

'Something new? I've often thought I should. I watch that programme, *Cook Up a Storm*. The stuff they use! Sun-dried tomatoes, cardamoms . . . I can't see my old man standing for that. Still, I did think, maybe. But I couldn't be bothered. What are you doing? Some people do flower-arranging. But you do the flowers for the house beautifully already.'

'No. Not flower-arranging. Actually, Mrs Bean, no one knows anything about it yet, so you won't say anything, will you? But I'm becoming a magistrate.'

'Well I never! Isn't that like a judge?'

'Not quite the same. I won't wear a wig.'

'I think you're ever so brave.'

'So do I! The thought scares me sometimes.'

'There's people in Swanmere going to have a surprise when it does come out,' said Mrs Bean. 'They won't believe you had it in you. That sounds rude. I don't mean it that way. But they just think of you as the lady who looks after everybody.'

Laura smiled ruefully, only too aware of how true that was.

## 5

Mrs Bean kept her mouth shut. But by the time Laura had been successfully appraised and taken her seat in court, this (to Mrs Bean exciting) event turned out to be of little moment in Swanmere.

Being on the whole a law-abiding population, the inside of a court and the work of its magistrates was a closed book to the village. Mrs Fortescue's disgrace had been a much-spoken of scandal – there were those who had 'always known' there was something fishy about the old lady – but all that had been forgotten with her death and burial.

As surprised at herself as she had been about her own doggedness in seeing the preliminaries through, Laura now surprised herself again by wishing that someone would be interested enough to come and see her at work.

However, she did not wish for an audience enough to mention her new position to her mother, who had long lost interest in anything outside of Cathay Manor, the luxury residence for elderly gentlefolk now privileged to have Mrs Chadwick as its queen regnant. Prior to her installation at the Manor, Veronica had been an ineluctable presence in Laura's house. During the long year she was there, Laura had not passed a day without being made to feel guilty about something. So it was a huge relief that Veronica, by her own choice, had moved into Cathay Manor, where all that was required of Laura was to listen and nod admiringly as her mother related tales of her own popularity.

Her days in court rapidly became a separate part of her existence, a whole different world from Swanmere, a world of the pitiable and the bad, of the mean-spirited and loose-fingered, of the dangerous and the endangered, of swindlers and liars of greater or lesser plausibility. She learnt the necessity of keeping her ears alert through long boring evidences in cases of DSS fraud, and cars of dubious ownership – 'Logbook? Got stole' – and no insurance.

Often, by the time she got home, she was almost speechless with exhaustion. Proud of her though he was, it was no part of her husband's remit to lift a finger in the house. She adored having her grandson to stay, and missed him hugely when he returned to his parents, but when little J. L. had a wakeful night (J. L. was a martyr to tigers under the bed) it was Laura who had to go to him. And baby J. L. was now with them quite a lot. Ann and her husband, Len, had achieved their great ambition, a restaurant of their own. For this reason, Laura deliberately played down the busyness of her new existence. She loved them both, and they both loved her. And the last thing in the world she could bring herself to do was anything that might jeopardise their new venture.

During the days Mrs Bean came to the rescue, coming in more frequently to look after J. L. Though a dear little boy, he was a great time-and-energy consumer, and Mrs Bean was not as young as she had been. As a result Laura frequently found herself, after a day in court – she spent at least one day a week there, sometimes two – not only cooking dinner but also doing a pile of ironing, and rapidly trying to dust the sitting room. She saw nothing odd in this.

Very occasionally she went into the court canteen for a cup of coffee. It amused her to see how young the female solicitors were, and how enviably self-assured. They were mostly married or in 'partnerships' but when she ventured to ask how they managed to run a home and a job with no apparent signs of undue fatigue, she found she had a lot to learn. 'Ironing? Me? No fear! My stuff's all drip-dry, and if Jimmy wants that sort of shirt, he can iron it himself.' Some of the Jimmies, it seemed, also did the cooking, otherwise it was Marks & Spencer and like it.

Peter Fenby, John and Laura's eldest, now lived in Venice. His escape there had not surprised Laura, but what had given her a real shock was when Judy, her number two child – the orderly Judy – had gone on holiday to stay with Peter there, then quit her job and stayed. Peter and Judy had always been seen by their mother as her quiet ones, but Judy, brilliant at her job had been rising steadily up the corporate ladder. She dressed well if discreetly, and always looked cool and unruffled. She had bought a small, extremely presentable flat, as self-contained as herself, and seemed to have it all going for her. But for some undefinable reason she had very little confidence in herself as a woman. Perhaps it was *because* she was so self-possessed, Laura thought, that she seemed to attract so many unsuitable men. They always had quite serious flaws in their characters, not immediately apparent, but coming pretty quickly to the surface, and Judy terminated these liaisons with dispatch. Perhaps she was just tired of the game.

'I hope,' said John, 'that she isn't going to do something foolish. I've nothing against Italian men, but I don't think I'd like to marry one.'

'I don't think you'll be asked to,' said Laura

'I meant Judy.'

It was Luke, the youngest, who told Peter and Judy their mother's latest news. Luke, whether he had money or not, always thought big, and was a great telephoner. He rang during a meal at the hotel where they lived.

'I say, Peter, what do you think? Mummy's a beak.'

'A what?'

'She's a magistrate. On the local bench. I promise you, it's true. Only think, she can send people down. Not me, thank God. If I – or anyone else she knows – get done for dangerous driving, she's excused. But isn't it amazing? Would you ever have imagined her doing anything like that?'

Peter, thinking of his calm, loving, understanding mother, slowly took it in.

'You're right, it's extraordinary. But I'll tell you something: I'll bet she's good at it.'

'Do you think so? You may be right, but I can't think why she would have done it.'

'Now she's got rid of all of us, why on earth not? She and Father will be able to swap judicial jokes over dinner. Has it put his nose out?'

'No, I don't think so. He just looks a bit bemused, that's all.'

'He always looks like that. How's Mary? Dare I ask, are you still with her? And you, are you all right?' Peter had always liked Luke's pretty divorcee.

'Fine, thanks, and still with Mary, sort of. I mean, she'll drop me like a stone if she gets a millionaire, but we're having a great time at the moment. How's Judy?'

'Judy is very well, and relaxed, and she's just finished a superb plate of pasta. Which is frankly, chum, what I'd like to go back and do. Ciao, and love to everyone. Especially Mum. And my congratulations to her, too.'

Peter had found a way of living that seemed to suit him. He had simply arrived in Venice and moved into a small hotel. As weeks went by, he'd felt no compulsion to move. He was not exactly happy, but homelessness suited him right now. He lived cheaply and had sufficient money for the moment. When Judy came out to stay with him, she took another room in the same hostelry. When she decided to stay on she quit her job and sold her flat in London, so she had enough money to last her for a while.

'For a while' became their tenet. They were both unsettled, for different reasons, reasons known only to each other.

The proprietor had at first thought that Judy was Peter's girlfriend. They were sufficiently different to look at not to be taken for brother and sister. He was surprised at the request for a separate room. Although quite old enough to remember the days of virtuous behaviour, Signor Pizzero was also sharp enough to adapt.

He had already grown to like the shy, bespectacled

Englishman who had come to Venice because he loved the city, and now also thought him old-fashioned. But no, this really was the sister, Miss Fenby. They paid their bills regularly, at the end of each week, and they usually dined together.

For his part, Peter enjoyed going about Venice with his sister. Judy aroused enormous notice. Her smooth and impeccable blonde hair and her slim figure made it impossible to go far without notice being taken. If they sat down at a pavement café table, she was immediately approached.

'Are you American?'

'No.'

'Australian?'

'No. I'm English.'

'Is this your husband?'

'No, he is my brother.'

The Venetians found this hard to believe.

And so Peter and Judy whiled away their days, neither quite restless nor fulfilled, each quietly supporting the other.

# 6

The spring rain was pattering monotonously on the glass roof of the courtroom. Laura was thankful it was not a dull case that was before them, as they had already had a full morning and it was now the beginning of an afternoon session.

It was a far from dull case. The magistrates had in the dock a local man whose recent activities had led him to incarceration in Maidstone Prison, from which he had to be brought for today's hearing. Among other antisocial activities, he had battered half to death the woman who had been so unwise as to take up residence with him.

The court was full. The story had attracted considerable notice, so not only were most of the public seats occupied, but those of the press as well. However Laura took little notice of this, giving all her concentration to the case, listening to the solicitors and to the police statements. The case took up the whole afternoon. Even so, it was not resolved and the defendant was remanded.

By the time the magistrates rose, they were all extremely tired and anxious to get home. Laura was putting her car key in the lock when she heard herself addressed by name.

'Mrs Fenby? May I have a word with you?' The man who spoke was of average height and wearing a completely conventional suit, white shirt and a tie with diagonal stripes which Laura was later to learn were the stripes of the Artillery. With a frankness amounting to naïvety he added, 'I'm from the *Mid-County Express*. I'm a journalist.'

Meeting courtesy with courtesy, Laura made her reply polite but firm. 'Absolutely not, I'm afraid. I'm sorry, but it's out of the question. You'll have to make do with what you can get in court. You must know that, as a magistrate, I couldn't possibly discuss this or any other case with a journalist.'

'It wasn't the case I wanted to ask you about. I was watching you on the bench, and I was fascinated by such powers of concentration. What made you become a magistrate?'

'I–' Laura began, but stopped herself in time. She was not going to be wheedled into something that would certainly turn out to be a fatal indiscretion. 'Excuse me, I really must go.' She got into her car, fastened her seat belt, closed the door rather more roughly than was her usual wont, reversed, turned sharply, and drove away.

The next morning, as Laura was playing with little J. L., in order to free Mrs Bean and let her get on with the cleaning for which the house was crying out, the telephone rang. 'Mrs Fenby? Nott here, David Nott. *Mid-County Express*.'

This time, Laura said goodbye to courtesy. 'Mr Nott, you have no right to bother me in this way. I've told you I cannot speak to you, and that is final.'

'Look, I'm a cub reporter. An elderly cub reporter,

I admit. Just listen a minute, please. I'm doing a feature on the empty nest syndrome. And I saw you as a sparkling example, a role model you might say, of what a woman can do with her life when her children are gone.'

Intrigued, in spite of her annoyance, Laura now said, 'And how come you know that much about me? Whatever way, you have an infernal nerve.'

'Well, everyone knows who your husband is. And he's listed in the telephone book under your home number as well as his office number. He's had a successful partnership for many years, so it's a reasonable supposition that you are old enough to have grown-up children.'

Laura burst out laughing. 'You've got the most colossal cheek. You've seen how old I am and I refuse to be flattered, and I'm certainly not letting you talk me into being part of your article, so that is that. And while we're at it, may I ask how you come to be a cub reporter at your time of life?'

'I was in the army. I retired a couple of years ago. I couldn't think what to do with myself at first. Funnily enough, I loved the countryside and walking and I started writing down bits about what I saw. Then I met a bloke in a pub, who turned out to be the Editor of the *Mid-County Express*. He took a look at the pieces and bought them, and now they like me enough that I sort of belong there. I think they let me cover the court cases because I've got one good suit.'

'And you look respectable. Well, I'm not going to be coerced, however respectable you may look.'

'All right, then. But you could help me, if you would be so kind. If I promise faithfully not to mention your name, would you meet me one day and let me ask you what other women like you do at this stage of their lives? You must have friends like yourself, who are making a second life. And, after all, it's what I'm doing. So be a sport, dear Mrs Fenby, and have lunch with me.'

'When?' asked Laura, horrified at herself.

'Today? I could pick you up in half an hour. No one need see you speaking to me. I know a pub miles away.'

'I can't. I've got to give my grandson his lunch,' said Laura austerely.

'I can hear a vacuum cleaner. That means you've got someone there, so you won't have to leave the child alone.'

When David Nott parked outside the Grange, J. L. was happily accepting spoonfuls of food from Mrs Bean, of whom he was now so fond that he scarcely noticed the difference between Granny and Beany.

On the way to the pub Laura, for once having the luxury of being driven, enjoyed looking out of the window at the delicate green of the spring trees, the hedgerows, and the shapely winding of the lanes they traversed.

'Would you like a glass of wine? I won't, not because I don't but because I'm driving.'

'I won't either,' said Laura, resolving to keep her wits about her. She had not looked at David Nott on the drive to the pub. Now she noticed that he was wearing jeans more suited to a younger man, although he certainly did not bulge in them. His Jermyn Street shirt was one which must have gone downhill to gardening status. He had rather small features, nothing like as good-looking as her husband, and bright blue eyes of which the whites were as smooth and clear as a child's. Even so, he required glasses to look at the menu. 'I'm going to have the ploughman's. What about you? Omelette? Prawn salad? Scampi in a basket?'

'I'll have the ploughman's too.' The sooner this was over and done with, the better, she decided.

'If it's ploughman's,' said David, 'I think I'll allow myself one glass of beer. Will you change your mind and have something?'

'All right. I'll have a beer, then.'

The soft roll was awful, the pickled onion acid, the cheese greasy, the brown chutney chokingly vinegary. Laura said, 'I can't really think, offhand, of much about what other women do. I have a friend who started a sort of business giving children's parties, but it wasn't much of a success. But I'll try and think. What about you? Are you married?' she asked abruptly.

'Yes.'

'And your wife? Has she an empty nest? It's your expression, not mine.'

'We have a son and a daughter. Our son is in India, and our daughter is in Australia.'

'So what does your wife do, to fill her days?'

'She is not very well, unfortunately.'

'I'm sorry.' Laura could do no more with the dismal ploughman's. 'I really must get back. My daily is already doing more than she should, giving my grand-son his lunch. Have you got grandchildren?'

'Not that I know of.'

The day before's rain had given way to the sort of bright March sunshine that lures animals and humans into believing that winter is past. The hedgerows were full of primroses and aconites. 'Do you mind if we stop for a moment?' They had reached a narrow bridge over a stream. David got out of the car. 'I used to play Pooh-sticks here, with my sister, when we were little.'

'My children never would. I tried to show them how.'

David wandered down under the bridge. Laura thought he must want to pee, and modestly averted her gaze. 'I think these water irises will soon be in flower,' he said. 'Come and look.'

'I can see from here. Anyway, it's too early for them. June, at the very soonest.'

He came back and got into the driving seat. On the return journey they talked only of the article he was about to write.

Mrs Bean, looking out of the window, saw Mrs Fenby get out of a car and shake hands with a gentleman she didn't know. Well, she would be meeting a lot of new people with her work, wouldn't she?

# 7

That afternoon, Laura went to see her mother. Driving up to Cathay Manor, she managed to brace her courage by reminding herself that three or four hours a week were a dream in comparison with the day-in, day-out strain of having Veronica living with them. It didn't stop her from feeling guilty, nor allow her to admit, even to herself (most of all, not to herself) that her mother was a selfish, manipulative bully and that she had been frightened of her all her life.

Veronica was seated in the drawing room, *The Times* open at what she now complained was the remnants of any sort of a decent Court page, now that the younger royals had married harlots and vulgarians. Laura had brought a bunch of early daffodil buds and polyanthus from her garden. While she was there, they wilted away untouched.

'What do you do with yourself these days?' asked Veronica. 'You never come to see me.'

'I come as often as I can, Mummy. I was here on Sunday. Perhaps you forgot.'

'I don't forget anything. I just hardly ever see you.'

Laura was about to use little J. L. as an excuse, but she was damned if she would sell her beloved grandson down the river, nor yet Ann and Len. Veronica had always despised Len, and Ann for marrying him. 'I'm in court quite a lot,' she said.

'In court? What do you mean by that? What on earth are you in court for?'

'I'm a magistrate.'

'You didn't tell me. But then, nobody really bothers to tell me anything, since you shoved me in here to get me out of the way.'

'Mummy, really, that's not fair. We did not "shove you in here", as you put it. You can't have forgotten. You came and saw it the day you and Deirdre went out together, and you liked it. It was your choice to come here.'

'Deirdre? What's happening about Deirdre and Peter? Peter going off to Venice like that. He must have been mad. I was very fond of Deirdre and she was an excellent wife to him. Almost made a man out of him.'

Laura remembered how well Veronica had got on with Deirdre and also how much she herself had distrusted the girl and rapidly changed the subject. 'I only didn't tell you about me becoming a magistrate because I wasn't sure whether I'd make it or not.'

'I can't imagine you a magistrate. You've no qualifications for anything like that. You've never even had a job.'

'I quite agree, Mummy, that's just what I thought. But apparently the selectors thought differently. So I am a magistrate, for better or for worse.'

'Your father was a magistrate. But that was a different thing. He was a marvellous man, a brilliant soldier, brilliant at everything he did.' Veronica's reminiscences had become a happy cloud of lies. Now, her late husband had risen in glory to the position of lover and genius. She had quite forgotten her midlife behaviour, during which she had cuckolded the poor man with all and, indeed, sundry, from the gardener to the double-glazing fitter. She now went on to enquire, 'How are the children?' with the inevitable rider that they never came to see her.

Laura explained patiently, 'Peter and Judy are in Venice together, as you know,' privately resolving to get hold of those two and threaten them with excommunication if they didn't immediately write to their dear granny. 'Ann always asks after you. They are very busy with the new restaurant. And Luke. You've seen Luke quite recently, haven't you?'

Luke had rung to tell her he'd been to see Granny and taken her out to a slap-up lunch: 'Granny can't half put it away!'

'Oh well, I suppose I have, if you say so. Why doesn't Marion Clark ask me over to lunch, any more? That was one thing I used to enjoy. She always did everything so well.'

'She went to America, with Jeremy. Don't you remember?' It was difficult, sometimes, to decide whether her mother was becoming senile, or simply exercising her life-long talent for ignoring anything that didn't suit her.

'I remember everything. If I am told, that is. But no doubt you thought that it wasn't worth bothering to tell me that a woman who was such a kind friend to me had left the country.'

To Laura's relief they were now joined by Miss Fawcett-Smythe, the elderly spinster who prided herself on being Cathay Manor's resident flower-arranger, a skill acquired during endless, long-ago years as an unmarried daughter. She was half hidden by a bushel of evergreens, and spoke from behind them. 'Oh, dear Veronica, you have a visitor. Don't let me interrupt family business. I'll come back later.'

'Nice to see you again, Miss Fawcett-Smythe. How are you?' Laura wished the old girl wouldn't go.

'Splendid, thank you, very well indeed,' said Miss Fawcett-Smythe, a response she would eventually give on her deathbed.

At dinner that evening, Veronica was joined at table by Miss Fawcett-Smythe, a Mrs Henry, and two of Cathay Manor's sparse supply of gentlemen, Major Tomkins and Mr Simpson. Sparkling in male company, Veronica announced, 'I don't know whether I told you, but my daughter has become a magistrate. I was surprised in a way. It's not a thing I could do in a million years, I'm far too sensitive. But of course her father, my dear late husband, was a magistrate, so I suppose she takes after him. So sad I couldn't give him a son. But alas, I was so delicate. However, he would have been so proud of Laura. She's really turned out quite well. And, of course, she's a wonderful mother.'

Miss Fawcett-Smythe drooped in pathetic admiration of Veronica, wife, widow, mother and grandmother, all status symbols denied her from the day of her birth to a mother not unlike her dear friend.

Going home, Laura resolved that tonight's dinner should not be something she'd got out of the freezer. She bought two chicken breasts, and took trouble to make a béchamel sauce to serve with them. She also made a treacle tart, one of John's favourites. Then she spent half an hour bathing and playing with J. L., and read to him from *Little Black Sambo*, reflecting that hers must be the last house in England to have such subversive literature on its nursery shelves. She very much hoped she would live to introduce him to *Just William*, and eventually *Stalky & Co*.

At dinner, she told her husband something about the interesting case upon which they had sat on Monday. In the middle of doing so, she remembered that she had said nothing about being approached by the journalist David Nott, nor that she had been out to lunch with him. She decided that it wasn't really a matter of any interest to John. Anyway she would almost certainly never see David Nott again, except maybe from her seat on the bench, should he be covering further court stories. Yet at the back of her mind nagged the fact that the omission was both deliberate and spontaneous.

David Nott, whose home was a serviceable but cheerless flat on the outskirts of a county town whose former coaching charm had been overwhelmed by precincts and hideous fascias, was also silent about his day's activities. There was, alas, no point in telling Fiona anything. Although 'the poor girl' was no older than him, she was already in the early stages of Alzheimer's. He had been warned by the doctor that her irrational and forgetful behaviour was very likely the onset of this dread disease, but had so far tried to convince himself that it was only prolonged menopausal symptoms, and would, one day, be over. She had, after all, always been highly strung. Even the supposedly joyous business of having babies had only

37

frightened and depressed her. She hadn't even got any fun out of their begetting. However lovingly and gently he tried, he had never been able to arouse in her the slightest pleasure. He felt guilty about taking his pleasures elsewhere, and had always gone to elaborate lengths to ensure that Fiona knew nothing about that.

# 8

There was no immediate need to worry about seeing David Nott again, even in court. Laura's next two sittings were in Youth Court so, no public, no press. And, almost invariably, no parents. Child offenders coming before the court were, it appeared, well supplied with social workers and probation officers, but less fortunate when it came to parental care.

Laura was shocked by the appearance of an eleven-year-old boy who could have been Luke at that age. And by a thirteen-year-old girl who looked not unlike either of her own daughters at that age, except that neither of them had been seven months pregnant when they were thirteen.

The boy was a thief. Luke, at eleven years old, had pinched the small change off the kitchen dresser – 'It was just lying there, Mummy. I didn't think it was anybody's.' Laura had explained that it was her money, earned by Daddy, to which he'd replied, 'Well then, you and Daddy have got lots of money, and I haven't got any,' a point of view now put forward by the child before her.

This eleven-year-old had robbed a pensioner. 'There was lots of money in her flat, and I hadn't got any,' he explained. The difference between him and

Luke was that he had given the old woman a black eye and smashed in her teeth. 'So what? They were only false ones and she can get more free.'

The pregnant girl had been sleeping rough and begging, having been turned out by her third soi-disant stepfather. Later on Laura learnt, through a newspaper to which the mother had sold her story, that this loving parent was preparing to sue the education authorities for not providing adequate sex instruction. 'Sex instruction,' said John Fenby cynically, 'she seems to have managed without.' Laura was glad to note that the paper was a national, and not David Nott's *Mid-County Express*.

She couldn't help wondering about David Nott. How strange for him not even to know whether he was a grandfather.

At about this time her own grandson, J. L., became unwell. A sniffy cold turned into something like flu. Ann, distraught, left Len to look after their restaurant, and rushed home to the Grange. Poor darling, she wasn't much help. Laura felt she had two infants on her hands, one coughing and crying, and the other crying and crying, and Len perpetually on the telephone.

Next, Veronica had an attack of chest pains. At Cathay Manor you could have a day in bed with a chill, but anything smacking of feet first out of the back door meant hospitalisation.

Between convalescent J. L. (and the usually sunny little boy was as cross as two sticks: 'I feel sick. I'm gonna *be* sick') and hospital visiting, Laura gave no further thought to her new acquaintance.

She visited the hospital twice a day. At first she had

thought her mother was dying. She was unaccountably filled with sorrow at the prospect. Now that Veronica was no longer living under her own roof, Laura had developed a sort of admiration for the indomitable old harridan. She hated to see her so quiet, so pale, plugged into frightening machines, covered with wires and stickers, half-naked and lost to the dignity which meant so much to her.

She spoke to her very gently. 'Mummy? How are you feeling?'

'Terrible. It must have been food poisoning.' There was to be no talk of coronaries from Veronica Chadwick. 'We had prawns in aspic for lunch. Don't ever mention prawns to me again. There's a lot wrong there, you know. But I mustn't complain. I went there to suit you, and I'll stick it out.' The bravery of this relentless dishonesty was almost lovable.

'Just get well,' said Laura. 'We can make different arrangements if you'd prefer. Do you want to come to us for a while?'

'I don't want to be in the way. But of course, it would leave what there is of my poor little income for you, when I die.'

'Mummy, please don't talk about dying.'

Getting her car out of the car park, Laura was surprised almost to bump into David Nott. 'Mrs Fenby, mind my headlights.'

She pulled up alongside his car and wound down her window. 'I'm so sorry, I was a bit distracted. I've been visiting my mother. What brings you here?' She remembered he had said something about his wife's health not being good.

'I'm doing a story on volunteer workers in hospital. Marvellous women. They varnish people's nails, you know. Stuff like that.'

'How interesting.'

'Not very. But it's the sort of thing I make a few bob out of doing. And the older readers like it. We get letters saying how nice it is to hear that there is still some good in this wicked old world. Come and have a coffee.'

John, Laura thought, having reparked her car and joined David Nott, could not possibly mind, even if he knew she was sitting in the hospital coffee shop with another man. David Nott was not especially good-looking.

'You look weary,' he said, so he wasn't playing the flatterer today, either.

'I am. I'm exhausted.'

'The bench?'

'No. Other things. I'm really quite glad to get to court. It takes my mind off it. I have a grandson at home, plus his mummy. My grandson is getting over one of those things little children get that frighten you out of your wits. And his mum, my daughter, is beside herself.'

'And your mother is in here?'

'Yes. I thought she was dying.'

'You poor thing.' David put a bony hand on hers. A great wave of tangible sympathy seemed to shoot up her arm and into her chest. 'Are you very close to your mother?'

'Not really, no. But she is my mother. And it made me sad to see her frightened, even though she pretends she isn't.'

A young woman with enormous thighs stuffed to bursting point into overstretched tights passed by. She was carrying a plateful of pastries, several bars of chocolate, and a cup of milky coffee into which she now poured three packets of sugar.

'I sometimes think I should go on a diet,' said Laura, feeling despondent in this depressing place.

David burst out laughing. 'I hardly think that's necessary,' he said. They finished their coffee and returned to the car park.

'It was really nice to see you,' he added. 'Have lunch with me again some time, if you'd like to?'

'No, I don't really have time for lunching out. I tell you what, though, why don't you and your wife come and have dinner with us one night? May I telephone her and ask her?'

'No, thank you so much all the same. But I'm afraid she's not up to it.'

Veronica was in the hospital for another week, after which Laura took her home to the Grange for a while to recuperate. To save the household trouble, Veronica tottered downstairs at ten o'clock every morning, and spent the rest of the day on the drawing-room sofa. Laura gave her a little bell to ring if she needed anything. But Veronica resolutely refused to use it, with the result that Laura felt obliged to drop whatever she was trying to do and go in to her every half-hour, to see if she was all right, and not being pestered by J. L. Ann did her best to help, but mostly she wished Granny would get back to Cathay Manor.

'It's too much for you, Mum,' she said, 'but who am I to talk, selfish cow that I am? Once the restaurant begins to pay, I'll be able to get an au pair, and take him off your hands.'

'But I love having him here, and he's used to me now.' Laura was unable to say less than this to her beloved daughter. It was unthinkable that Ann should feel for one moment that she was incommoding her mother. Laura had been subjected, by Veronica, to far too much guilt for that. 'I don't like the idea of him going to a stranger. Mightn't it be better, if you and Len can afford it, to get extra help in the restaurant to let you look after him, at least until he's through nursery school?'

Ann burst into tears. 'But Len can't manage the restaurant without me. Oh, Mum, I'm so sorry. I feel so guilty about it all.'

'Well, don't!'

It came as a relief when Luke, early in April, turned up for a weekend visit, bringing Mary with him. As she was well aware that Luke and Mary had been cohabiting for the last two years, Laura hastily made up the spare double bed. Much to her surprise, Mary demurred. 'I'm sure we shouldn't, in your house.'

'Oh, Mary, dear, really. What do you mean?'

'Well, we're not married. I thought you'd think it wasn't proper. My father wouldn't allow it. He found my young brother in bed with his girlfriend and he threw them both out of the house at three o'clock in the morning.'

Mary's father, Laura knew, was a peppery septuagenarian, and well behind the times, even for that age. Oh my God, she thought sadly, I feel so bloody old.

# 9

In the end Mary insisted that she and Luke spent their two nights at the Beaters' Arms. They were already popular with the landlord and his wife, Betty, having stayed there before.

'Same room, then?' said Betty. 'How's your mother, Luke? I thought she looked tired, last time I saw her out shopping.'

'Not surprising, she's got Granny staying, poor Mum. Granny's had some sort of a heart attack. Well, I suppose it proves she's got a heart, though you could have fooled me.'

'Luke, that's no way to speak about your grandmother.' But Betty grinned. She had seen quite enough of Mrs Chadwick to wonder how it was possible for such a sweet lady as Mrs Fenby to be her daughter.

'I think Laura's marvellous, don't you?' said Mary. 'How she manages to do all she does, and be a magistrate as well, I don't know.' Betty nodded, but, like almost everyone else in the village, Mrs Fenby's position as a magistrate meant very little to her. Her boundary was Swanmere, and what people did outside of that was of no interest compared to speculations as to whether Tesco was going to be allowed in, who was expecting, hip replacements and hysterectomies and who had fallen out with whom.

'Are you going to marry me?' asked Luke, in bed later.

'And lose my alimony?'

'Bollocks. You don't get alimony.' Mary had come out of her youthful divorce owning a flat and nothing else. Her quite substantial income was earned by her. 'I'm in love with you, darling.'

'Oh, Luke, not that again. I know you are, and I love you too. We have a fine and lovely time together. There's no need to go getting married.'

'Please, I want us to have children.'

Mary laughed. 'You've been playing with J. L. and it's made you broody. But it would be a very different thing to have one of our own. You're not lazy, I know you're not, but you'd have to keep a job. Because if I ever have children I won't go out to work any more, I can tell you. I have no intention of being a latch-key mother.'

'That sounds as though you disapprove of Ann.'

'Me? Disapprove of anybody? I'm more used to being disapproved of. But I do think Ann is missing out, and she may regret it later. No, Luke, no baby.'

'In a while, maybe?'

Mary changed the subject. 'How's Peter?' she asked.

'He's fairly all right, I think. He and Judy get on well together, in their funny way. I'm glad she went out and joined him. It might loosen her up a bit, and it means he's not so lonely as he was.'

When they woke up in the morning, it was pouring with rain and blowing a gale. The windows in the bedrooms of the Beaters' Arms were long overdue for renewal. They rattled dismally, rain came in through the frames and soaked the curtains Betty had made many years ago when she and her husband first came to the pub. She had bought the material for them cheaply, in the market. Brown and orange had not been a very attractive colour combination, even then, and now, sodden and flapping, they were a dreary sight. Mary lay in bed, wishing there was an en suite bathroom and wishing she was back in London.

At the Grange Laura took breakfast up to her mother's room, wondering whether Veronica would ever choose to return to Cathay Manor. J. L.'s cold seemed to have reasserted itself now that Ann had gone back to Len and their restaurant. J. L.'s nose was streaming and he refused to learn to blow and yelled when Laura tried to wipe it.

John Fenby went to church. The service might have taken longer if the prayers for the Royal Family had not become so curtailed, most of its younger members now being past praying for.

'No Laura today?' said Theodore Carew after the service, bravely forcing himself out of the porch and bearing the wind and rain on the vestments so recently ironed by Dorothy.

'She's still looking after her mother.'

'Poor Veronica, I saw her in the hospital, but I must pop round and see if she would like me to bring her communion. All well, otherwise, I hope? Laura well?'

'Yes, very well, thank you. Our grandson has a cold.'

★

In his flat David Nott said to his wife, 'I'm afraid I won't be able to take you out today, dear, the weather is too bad.'

'Where are we going?' asked Fiona.

'We can't go anywhere. It's too wet, and blowing a gale.' He brought her some coffee, but she didn't quite know how to lift the cup. So he switched on the television, and tried to get on with his article about volunteer workers in hospitals. Laura Fenby kept coming into his mind. He envied her husband.

He held the cup to Fiona's mouth, then wiped her chin and took her to the bathroom. On the way back to her chair, Fiona asked, 'Where did we go?'

'Nowhere,' said David.


The weather in Venice was cool but bright. Peter and Judy Fenby wandered round St Mark's Square. Tourists were assembling, but they were still the respectful sort who come early in the year to Venice.

The Fenbys sat at an outdoor table drinking coffee. 'I couldn't help hearing you speaking English,' said a tall American who was flicking his fingers in an effort to order some refreshment from a waiter who thought nothing of him. 'Do you speak this lingo too? I ought to. My grandfather was Italian, but I've never learnt.'

'My brother does,' said Judy. 'I'm learning, but I haven't got very far.'

'You are brother and sister?' He had thought they were husband and wife. 'My name is Larry Cunningham. I'm from Chicago. I am recently divorced.'

'So is my brother,' said Judy, falling rapidly into this tell-all, easy-going demeanour.

'And you?'

'I,' said Judy, 'am another story.'

Larry Cunningham perceived before him a very good-looking blonde, as well-groomed as any American woman. He flattered himself upon recognising British reticence and went slowly, only confining himself to a request that Peter and Judy might take pity on him, join him for lunch and show him the town.

For the first time since leaving her London life behind her, Judy was reacquainted with what money could buy and, again for the first time, not her own money. Larry was obviously well off, and, Peter having discreetly excused himself from regular outings, enjoyed escorting a pretty and elegant woman about, and particularly watching heads turn when he took her to the smarter bars and restaurants.

He, too, had a new experience. For all the temptations in the shops, Judy showed no desire to be bought presents. She did allow him to buy her one small crystal tortoise. 'My little sister, Ann, had a tortoise when we were young. She was always getting into trouble because she would have it in the house and it made messes on the sitting-room carpet.'

'Did your mother get mad?'

'No, not Mummy. She hardly ever got mad.'

Larry insisted on trips by gondola, a luxury in which Judy had never indulged before. She thought the gondoliers were ridiculous, but Larry enjoyed it, and she was having a nice time with a nice man.

Although Larry had announced his divorced status the very moment he introduced himself, Judy's reticence about her own life rapidly affected him and, beyond telling her that he had a son and a daughter, he said no more about his family, or anything about the hellish and destructive divorce he had gone through.

Judy no longer thought in terms of relationships. Relationships were something that had never worked out for her. For a brief while, when her younger sister Ann had married so happily and had her baby, Judy had striven to do the same. A year the elder, a competitiveness had entered into her life, and had led to the overeagerness which, in its turn, brought doom.

But she and Larry Cunningham were just two people going about together in a beautiful city. Judy had given up all contemplation of long-term happiness, and Larry had no intention of getting involved, ever again.

The Hotel Iris, in its quiet backwater, had served its inexpensive evening meal to its mainly back-packer clientele, and long ago locked its doors for the night.

Judy slept quietly in her single room. She had been out all evening, and come home very late. Her lady-like demeanour had earned her the privilege of her own key to the front door. She had had dinner with Larry Cunningham. She was not in love. But she had been to bed with him, which she had enjoyed very much. She had not had a period since leaving London, so she knew it was safe. However she had not expected that she would do such a thing. Larry, well-educated and well-dressed, had considerably better manners than most of her London circle. He had taken her hand to assist her on and off vaporetto or gondola. He had caught hold of her once when she slipped, and held her for a few moments. He had, while walking with her through St Mark's Square, put his arm round her, laid his face on the top of her head and then given her a quick kiss.

This evening, they had dined at his hotel. 'Will you come to bed with me?' he'd asked.

It had been a long time since Judy had been to bed with anyone. 'Yes,' she said.

Up in his bedroom, Larry had very gently stroked her hair back, and she had touched his slightly jowled face with kind fingers. They undressed in silence and without shyness. Larry's body, though no longer very young, was lean and fit. They entered the bed almost formally, and there found great pleasure.

Afterwards, Judy had bathed and dressed in a bathroom the like of which was unheard of at the Hotel Iris. Larry then called for a water taxi, told it to wait while he escorted her safely to the front door, where he kissed her good night, or rather, good early-morning.

She had always been used to getting her own taxis. Indeed, in London, her taxi account had frequently been used by her guests. Tonight's experience was extremely agreeable, but she had no intention of getting into the habit of it.

# 10

At last Veronica had gone back to Cathay Manor. Little J. L. was the innocent cause of her departure. Making her own bed and cleaning her own room, while Mrs Bean was preoccupied with the little boy's welfare, was not to Veronica's taste.

'I don't want to be a trouble to anyone,' she said, 'so I'll go. Don't worry about me, I'll be all right.'

'But you like it at Cathay Manor,' said Laura.

'Not really, but it can't be helped. I don't mind being lonely. After all, I scarcely see you *here* these days.'

Nor, he sometimes felt, did John Fenby. Although he should have known better, he had not really prepared himself for the amount of time Laura was now spending on her new commitment. There was a lot more to it than sitting one day a week in court.

In one week, Laura was away for three days attending a seminar. On the second evening of this she said to her husband, as she stooped over the ironing board, and the potatoes for supper boiled to a mush, 'For goodness' sake, John, couldn't you buy yourself some drip-dry shirts?'

At this point the potatoes boiled over, and John

rushed to the stove, but failed to switch off the gas before a few splashes of boiling water flipped over and landed on J. L.'s pudgy hand. J. L. had recently gone completely off bedtime, and now sat, rigid on the floor, roaring with pain and outrage, eyes and nose streaming.

'Stop it, J. L.,' snapped Laura, and added to her husband, 'Can't you wipe his nose?'

John Fenby had never in his life wiped a child's nose, and the sight of what was emerging from that of J. L. made him feel physically sick. J. L. wiped his own nose, on his grandfather's trouser leg.

In all her married life, even when under the stress of having her mother living with them, Laura had never spoken quite as acidly as this to her husband. After all, it wasn't his fault that she had spent more than thirty years of her life waiting on him with such vigorous hand and foot that he didn't even know that beds were only comfortable because someone put clean sheets on them, or that washing machines had to be loaded and unloaded and their contents ironed. It was her own doing that the replacement of a roll of lavatory paper was beyond his mechanical skills.

She mashed the potatoes, though they scarcely needed mashing, filled J. L.'s bawling mouth with a piece of chocolate, and carried him up to bed.

The following evening she was greeted on her return by Mrs Bean, saying, 'I can't think what happened to his poor little hand. Two blisters! I took him down to the doctor's. I was worried, you see. They said it looked like a scald. I got some ointment.'

Laura was utterly riddled with guilt. At her next court sitting, she found it difficult to concentrate. This morning she was in open court. She was so tired that she had to pinch her wrists to keep her attention alert. The court was filled with the friends of those who came into the dock. Young drug addicts and thieves were apparently better off for friends than they had been for parents in their Youth Court days.

She did not observe the section reserved for the press. So she was surprised to be greeted on the way to her car by David Nott.

'What brings you here?' she asked.

'That young man, your third case, the one who had all the drugs stashed behind the tiles in his bathroom – he's a local. His father was killed in the Falklands. Are you all right? You look extremely tired. Can I buy you a drink?'

'No. Thank you, but no. I'm driving. And in any case, I ought to get home. I've left Mrs Bean looking after J. L., and I've already done that far too often. Mrs Bean is my helper. J. L. is my grandson.'

'I know. You told me. And I've seen him. A dear little boy.' David Nott folded his arms and leant against Laura's car. 'It's not always easy, is it?'

'No, it is not. As a matter of fact, I'm beginning to think I shall have to give it up.'

'What are you planning to give up?'

'The magistracy, of course.'

'That would be a serious pity. In my opinion you are very good at it.'

Laura felt unaccountably elated. 'Look,' she said, 'I really have to get home. But perhaps you would like to follow me, and I could make us both a sandwich there. If you don't mind sharing it with a three-year-old. And a rather importunate one, at that.'

At Laura's kitchen table, David took the little boy up on to his lap and couldn't help wondering again if, somewhere in the world, he had a grandchild of his own.

'You're back early,' said Mrs Bean.

Laura, paranoically sensitive, imagined a criticism. 'Would you like to get off home, Mrs Bean?' she asked.

She had become so out of touch with her long-standing closeness to Mrs Bean that she had not realised, because she had not properly listened, that Mr Bean was now housebound with an arthritic hip, awaiting a replacement that was continually postponed owing to closed wards, crashed motor-cyclists, and his own refusal to shed the three extra stones of weight a lifetime of beer and ice cream had wrought. And she was not aware that a housebound Mr Bean was a bit of a crosspatch.

'No,' said Mrs Bean. 'If you're giving J. L. his lunch, I'll go up and finish the bedrooms.'

It was now the autumn of the year. 'Autumn,' said Laura, buttering bread, and slicing the remnants of last Sunday's chicken to make sandwiches, 'makes me feel guilty. It used not to.'

'Why does it now?'

'I've let the apples rot on the trees, not to mention the plums. I haven't made jam, or jelly, or anything.'

'Why should you? You have better things to do.'

'It's nice of you to say so.'

David put a piece of chicken sandwich into J. L.'s mouth. J. L. spat it out. 'No. Choccy,' he said.

'Is chocolate good for him?' asked David, as Laura went to the dresser and brought him a bar of

Cadbury's Dairy Milk. She could hear Mrs Bean moving about upstairs, obviously vacuuming as well as making beds. David continued, 'Your husband must be immensely proud of you.'

'Oh yes,' said Laura, 'he is. Would you like some coffee? I've only got instant. John doesn't like instant, and my mother always despised it. But I forgot to get anything else. I'm not a very good manager, I'm afraid.'

'My wife, Fiona, was a very good manager until she became unwell.'

'Poor her,' said Laura, thinking cancer.

'She has Alzheimer's,' said David bleakly.

He finished his coffee and rose to leave. He would have liked to kiss Laura Fenby, but it would not have been appropriate. He could not have coped with the cheek-by-cheek peck. Laura's mouth was beset a little by lines. But her chin was still firm enough to hold together the prettiness of her face. They shook hands.

After David had gone, Laura took J. L. up to have his after-lunch nap. A whole bar of chocolate turned out not to have been a good idea.

She was tidying magazines in the sitting room when he appeared. 'I've been sick in my bed. I've been sick on the stairs. And now I'm going to be sick in here.'

John chose this afternoon to come home early. 'We can't go on like this,' he said, walking away from the mess.

Mrs Bean went and got a bucket of water, disinfectant and a cloth. Coming backwards down the stairs on her knees, she suddenly let out a cry. 'My back!' She was weeping with pain, and bent double. Laura helped her on to the sofa, terrified of doing further damage.

Later, having taken Mrs Bean to the doctor, and then home with some painkillers, Laura wondered again if she should give up the magistracy. But much to her own surprise, towards the end of the day she found herself telephoning Ann.

'I'm terribly sorry darling, but I've got a problem. Mrs Bean has crocked her back.' Trying hard not to sound too abrupt, she added, 'I'm afraid we really can't cope with J. L. for much longer. If you can't afford an au pair, perhaps Daddy can help out with the money.'

'No need,' said Ann, in a stiff tone Laura had never heard before. 'I thought you liked having him. I'm sorry if it's a nuisance.'

Oh my God, don't tell me I'm going to fall out with my darling daughter. 'It's *not* a nuisance. It's just that I'm out a lot, with the court and everything.'

'I thought that was only once a week.'

'It is. But there are other things I have to do in connection. There's a lot I need to know, and there are meetings, and so on.' This was turning out to be the most difficult conversation Laura had ever had with any of her children. 'I know how hard you and Len are working, and how dependent he is on you. And I know it's not that you're less than a loving mum,' an awful pleading tone was entering in here. 'Maybe we could get an au pair here, but then that would hurt Mrs Bean's feelings.' Not hurting people's feelings had dogged most of Laura's life.

'We'll come and fetch him,' said Ann, who had never before snapped at her mother.

Laura could not explain any of what was on her mind to John. He would have been angry with what he would see only as Ann's irresponsible and selfish attitude. And she also imagined, almost morbidly, that he would despise her inability to cope with the sort of voluntary work other women did, as well as running impeccable homes.

In bed, half asleep, she thought of talking the whole thing over with David Nott. He was so easy to communicate with. She wondered whether she would ever see him again. He must, by now, be embarrassed at having let out the tragic truth of his wife's illness. She supposed he must once have been in love with her, as she herself had been with John. And, of course, still was.

Ann came alone to collect her little boy, because it was not possible for her and Len to leave the restaurant at the same time.

Laura went out and stood on the steps holding J. L.'s hand as the Land Rover drew up in front of the house. Ann had got thin and, unlike her sister, Judy, thinness did not become her. The last time Laura had seen Judy, she had been wearing an outfit that must have cost more than she, Laura, would have spent in six months. And Judy's smooth, fair hair bore all the comb-marks of the businesswoman's hairdresser. Ann's curly mop looked as though it smelt of cooking. Her unironed shirt had clearly never been worth attentive laundering in the first place.

'Who's that lady?' asked J. L.

Fortunately Ann did not hear this, so Laura picked up her grandson, held him tight, and put her arms round her daughter so that the hug could rub off.

Laura had put some lunch on the kitchen table. Defrosted prawns, a not-ripe-enough avocado, super-market tartare sauce, and brown bread that would have been nicer if it had not just been defrosted. J. L. put his finger in the sauce, poked some into his mouth, and made a face.

'He's upset because it's not ice cream,' said Mrs Bean. She had got all J. L.'s clothes clean and ready to pack, and bore them away upstairs. It had been decided that Ann should stay the night, and go home with her son in the morning.

Ann had never before seen such a sententious expression on Mrs Bean's face. She was unaware that backache was the cause of it. She felt guilty. And therefore a little cross. 'I'm sorry to be a nuisance, Mum.'

This slight resemblance to Veronica's way of speaking was very upsetting to Laura, especially as Ann was in no way the least like her grandmother, but a jolly, warm-hearted and generous girl who was simply in need of some temporary help.

'You're not a nuisance, don't talk nonsense. Having J. L. is a joy. It's only been tricky because I'm now involved in the bench. Maybe I shouldn't have done it, not until later.' This fruitless conversation went round in predictable circles for some time.

Finally Laura decided to change the subject. 'We haven't heard from Peter and Judy lately,' she said.

'I've heard from Judy,' said Ann. 'Peter's going to New York.'

'Nice place for a holiday. Are they both going? They could look up Marion and Jeremy.'

'Judy's not going,' said Ann. 'I'm not sure, but I have a feeling she's got someone in Venice. No, Peter's going alone.'

'Well, he could look up Marion and Jeremy. I'm sure they'd be pleased to see him.'

'Mum,' said Ann, 'don't you know about Peter and Marion?'

'I know he was always very fond of her.'

'Fond of her? Didn't you realise? Peter was madly in love with Marion. Still is, according to Judy.' At last she began to laugh. 'Mum, really, I hope you're a bit more observant as a beak.'

'What *are* you talking about?' asked Laura.

'Didn't you ever guess? That baby she lost, it was Peter's. It's a fact, I assure you. Judy found out about it. She and Pete were always close, and of course even more so now, while they've been living together in Venice.'

'How could I have been such an idiot?' said Laura.

That night, Ann went early to bed. The drive had tired her. Her usual driving was to get supplies for the restaurant, and the motorway frightened and exhausted her. By the time she had got the over excited J. L. into bed – he regarded her more in the light of a new playmate than a mother – she was almost too tired to eat her supper. Laura, ashamed of the paltry lunch she had served, had rushed out and bought steaks, so Ann did her best although meat was not her favourite food.

After Ann had gone up to bed, Laura made a fresh pot of coffee. 'John,' she said, 'I heard some news from Ann today.'

'Not another baby on the way?' asked her husband. 'If so, much as I love our daughter, it's not coming here. You can have a dog, if you'd like one, but no more babies, I beg.'

'Not Ann. But it is about babies. Did you know that that baby of Marion Clark's wasn't Jeremy's? It was Peter's.'

'Good God! I did suspect that there was something between them, I must admit, but I obviously didn't guess all. I thought it was just a part of what was going wrong with him and Deirdre.'

'Even at that you were more observant than I was. Apparently Judy knew all about it. And now Peter's going to New York.'

'The young idiot. It'll have to be put a stop to. I'll talk to him.'

'You can't. It's none of our business. I only want him to be happy. He and Deirdre are divorced, so he's a single man.'

'Marion Clark is not a single woman. She has an excellent husband. Jeremy has always supported her. She had no business to indulge in an affair with another man, and Peter had no business to be that man. I hate divorce, you know I do. That's why I won't handle divorce cases.'

In the ensuing weeks it came as a relief to Laura to get back into court. Drugs, lies, thieving, violence and swindling the DSS absorbed her dispassionate attention.

Court, she thought to herself, is a rest–cure in comparison with home life.

# 12

'There's a Mr Nott on the telephone,' said Mrs Bean, whose back, if not better, was not bad enough to keep her at home with Mr Bean's invalid's temper. That, she thought to herself, was the gentleman who was having lunch with Mrs Fenby the day J. L. had vomited all over the house and she herself had put her back out.

Laura went to the telephone.

'Mrs Fenby?' David was planning a further article. His first piece, on the empty nest syndrome, had met with considerable success – Laura had read and liked it – and had brought in a gratifying number of letters, which had done him a lot of good with the paper. He very much wanted to interview Laura again, which was why he approached with formality.

'Oh, yes.' Laura was pleased to hear his voice, and so sounded careless.

'It's about an article I'm doing for the paper . . .'

'Now, David,' the name slipped out, 'you know I can't talk to you about anything that's happening in court. You have your press seats, you'll just have to make do with that.'

'It's not about cases that I want to talk to you. I would, of course, want to mention that you are a

63

magistrate, but that's all. It is, quite simply, a piece about women who have found a way of life after their children have grown up.'

'But you've already done that,' said Laura.

'This is to be in greater depth, and includes women who gave up promising careers for their families' sake. I thought of a working title, "Second Chances". I've got one woman who gave up nursing to marry, before she qualified. She started in again as a probationer when she was over forty. She's rather fun. She found it hilarious that all the patients on her ward kept calling her "Sister", although the real sister didn't think it was very amusing. And I've got a woman who didn't finish her degree, and is starting again now. You will help me, won't you? I won't bother you too much. May I just start now by asking you a few questions?'

'David, look, I'm not the least use to you on this. I never had a career, I didn't give up anything clever to have a family. I did it because it was what I wanted to do, and I was glad to get the chance. I was an only child, of an unhappy marriage. I didn't see much of either of my parents, and I wanted it to be different for my children.'

'That's very interesting, too. Would you tell me a little about them?'

To her own surprise, lulled by the faceless telephone, Laura began, 'Well, Peter went away to boarding school quite early. I minded that very much. But in fact he was very happy. He'd been a bit overwhelmed by his sisters. And it wasn't until later that Luke, my youngest, went.'

'And the girls?'

'They went to a grammar school, a day school.'

'Not boarding school?'

'No, my husband is old-fashioned. He didn't think it necessary to pay for the girls' education. But they came out very well in the end. John's old school wasn't as good as it had been in his day, and the girls had an excellent headmistress at the grammar.'

'And now there's no one at home? Except your little grandson.'

'He's not here now. I couldn't cope. I felt very badly about it. I didn't even manage very well when my mother was here. I felt badly about that, too. She's old and not terribly well, and I should have been kinder. She can't help being the sort of woman she is. Instead of which I was constantly irritated and I hadn't the courage to take a tough line with her, so I just took it out on my poor husband.'

She thought sadly about Veronica, a woman who could engender admiration in many, but no real love in her own daughter.

Listening to Laura's account of her home life, David could not help but think of the contrast it made with his own. He had made this telephone call from the newspaper office. Usually, he worked at home as much as he possibly could. He felt obliged to do this, in spite of having daily help for his wife, Fiona. The difficulties were enormous. Poor Fiona (he hated his own reference to her as 'poor') wandered in and out of the little room in which he kept his typewriter and files, fiddling with things and compulsively folding pieces of paper into ever-smaller squares.

But the nights were the worst. Although Fiona had never happily shared a bed with him, she would now sometimes climb in beside him, as a lonely, frightened child would do.

The daily help, Alma, was no Mrs Bean. She was dandy at polishing the bath-taps, but rooms, under the aegis of her vacuum cleaner, became circular. The corners were clogged with fallen biscuit crumbs. She addressed Fiona by her Christian name. Fiona, although not very old in years, had always, being a senior officer's wife, had an almost pre-1914 attitude. Being addressed as Fiona rather than 'Mrs Nott' added to the confusion in her mind. She kept asking Alma who she was, vaguely and anxiously believing she had forgotten some cousin.

What Alma was good at was giving advice. 'When they go like that,' she kindly told David, 'best have them put away.'

This helpful suggestion was not acceptable to David Nott, who often wondered whether his wife's rapid degeneration was partly his fault. Their married life had been a surface of military acceptability, not so much loveless (he and Fiona had united in affection for their children when young) as sexless.

He had, and had had for years, a mistress. A silly, pretty, enjoyable woman, safely married to a non-army husband.

Now he was seared with guilt. He could, he was sure, not blame Fiona in the least for the sexual disaster that informed their life together. He had married her because she had all the outward and visible signs of being the right wife for a rising officer. She was well-bred, nice-looking in a modest way, and played a good game of tennis. He believed himself to have been clumsy, inept, ignorant of the right spots to touch, at the outset.

Even now, he knew so little about her. She had endured sexual intercourse as a means of procreation. She had been kind and forbearing with the children, driving them to school, having their little friends to tea, sewing nametapes on their school clothes and taking them riding whenever the family was stationed near a stables.

David's regiment had served abroad a good deal, during which time he had risen to the rank of Colonel. Now he wondered whether long years of rootlessness had contributed to Fiona's problems. Army quarters, even nice ones, were not one's own roof.

That she was now in the state of a bewildered child was surely not her fault. Nothing was her fault. Most of all, it was not her fault that David had never been in love with her.

He was certainly not in love with Susie. Nor was Susie in love with him. They simply suited each other. Their activity in bed was their only communication, a meeting of bodies, not minds.

Susie was a cheerfully greedy creature. She liked to be flown to Paris for dinner and shopping, an expensive outing that David was only just able to underwrite. He was not her only lover. He didn't mind that. He could not spend time away from Fiona to take her to New York, even if he could have afforded to. Someone else did that.

'None of this is for an article. I'm just talking in private, please,' said Laura.

'Of course.'

'I'm afraid I haven't been the slightest use to you. I'm not even one of those middle-aged women who wants to find herself, and have a new lifestyle.'

'An expression I detest,' said David.

'So do I, actually. I don't even know what it means. I must have been trying to talk newspaperese.'

'Well, don't. You're a lot more interesting when you talk in your usual way. Goodbye.'

Laura put down the telephone, suddenly sad at the abruptness of his farewell.

The following day she sat in court on a case where a woman of eighty, a widow with a family long departed, had been robbed and beaten by a pair of gallant louts who wished to be excused punishment on the grounds that their activities were necessary for they had their drug requirements to meet. They knew the old woman well enough for their own purposes, living, as they did, in the same high-rise block.

'But I do have nice neighbours as well,' she said. 'They're not all bad. Even some of the bad ones have good in them.'

# 13

Christmas Day found Peter and Judy Fenby together in Venice. Peter was short of money; the visit to New York had been a considerable expense. Judy, although her funds were holding out, had a reason for not being in a spending mood. So they dined together at their little hotel. By now, they were so much part of the place that, over Christmas, they helped out in the kitchen, and ate with the family.

So far, Peter had said very little about his trip. On his return, Judy had simply asked him, 'How was New York?'

'All right,' had been his reply.

'Did you get to see Marion?'

'Yes.' He'd then changed the subject to ask, 'Did you have a good time while I was away?'

'I'm working on my Italian. It's getting quite good.'

'How's Larry?'

'Larry? Oh, Larry. Larry's gone back to America.' There'd been no knowing, from the expression on Judy's face, what her feelings were about this. Peter had asked if she expected him to return, and had been answered by a shrug of the shoulders, and an enquiry as to the wellbeing of Marion and Jeremy Clark.

Peter had arrived in New York late on a brilliant October day. Before he left, Judy had told him that the Clarks now lived in an apartment block called East Side Plaza. (She'd got this from Luke who'd just happened to see Laura's address book open at the right page.) She had thought he was not listening when she mentioned the telephone number. Peter had had, all his life, a memory for numbers. And now, although he had not said a word about it, even to Judy, he knew perfectly well why he had come to New York.

A telephone call from Peter Fenby came as a complete surprise to Marion Clark. Of course she remembered, with affection, the Fenby family of which he was a member. She and Jeremy never now spoke of the baby that had been born dead. All that had been washed away as though it had never been, as though it was no more than having a tooth extracted from the middle of the mouth, after which the teeth on either side close over the gap.

'Peter? Oh, Peter Fenby. How very nice. How are you? How is your mother?'

Peter, who was trembling, answered only, 'Very well, I think. I haven't seen her for quite a while. I'm living in Italy now, in Venice. So is Judy.'

'And Deirdre?'

'All right, as far as I know. We're divorced, actually.'

Marion had a vague idea, some sort of recollection, that Peter and his wife were divorced. She went on to ask after Ann, Len and their baby son, and then after John and Luke. Throughout all this Peter rolled out the conventional replies, alone in his small hotel room, facing disaster. He thought of ringing off when

Marion, the ever-polite Marion, went on to say, 'How nice that you are here. Jeremy will like to see you. You must come over to dinner one night.'

'Are you sure?' He realised he had failed to evoke in her even the faintest hint of the intimacy from which he had never recovered.

'Of course I am. Let's say, this Thursday. Are you here on business? I do hope you can make it. I'd like you to meet some friends of ours, and they are coming that evening. Seven thirty for eight, if that's all right?' She spoke in the tone of one who was simply making an old acquaintance welcome in town.

All Thursday afternoon Peter walked the streets of New York. He recollected later these few days as surreal, as part of a dream. He wandered across Central Park and got lost on the West Side. It was ten minutes to eight by the time he rang the Clarks' doorbell.

Jeremy answered the door. His dark, curly hair was now almost entirely grey. He was slightly overweight. He had always been jovial, and still was, as he ushered Peter in. Marion came forward and put up her face for the statutory kiss on each cheek.

The apartment was a small-scale version of the interior of the beautifully appointed home in which the Clarks had lived in Swanmere. Peter had brought flowers. Marion thanked him, and put the bunch into a vase with no water, so that Peter had the dubious pleasure of watching them droop as the evening went by.

He was introduced to his fellow guests, 'Our great friends Peggy and Francis.' Marion, as meticulous as ever, had levelled up her dinner party by inviting a woman for Peter, a New York single called Bethany, who was doing well in futures, but whose biological clock was ticking loudly.

Peter learnt that Francis was a colleague of Jeremy's and that his wife, Peggy, was a doctor. 'And Peter is the son of my dear friend Laura, in England. Peter lives in Venice now.'

Peter felt dazed and inane as the conversation rumbled round the table. 'Venice, great. I've never been to Venice,' said Bethany.

'It's a wonderful city. My sister is living with me there.' Bethany was delighted that it was a sister and not a wife, but hoped that Peter was not gay. She had had enough of that.

They were eating duck à l'orange. 'Marion,' said Peggy, 'is without doubt the best cook in New York. And the only woman I know who does it all herself.'

'Heavens, Peggy, I have all the time in the world to do it.' The conversation swirled round Peter until he felt almost faint. In Swanmere Marion had been better dressed than most of the other women. Now she had added the groom and polish of the well-off New York wife.

'Not only have I never been to Venice,' said Bethany, 'but I've never been to England either. Tell me about it. Where is your home?'

'A village called Swanmere,' said Peter. A village in which he had grown up, and in which he had fallen in love with Marion Clark, the married woman he adored even as a boy. He closed his eyes for a moment, and was in her garden, the wild place where he had first taken her in his arms while the sun came up on a September morning, and where his forbidden child had been conceived. His poor baby, born dead, with all Swanmere's sympathy going out to Jeremy, who was, not surprisingly, believed to be its father.

'Are you all right, old boy?' asked Jeremy. 'You've gone a bit pale.'

'I'm fine, thank you. Your martini was a bit strong.' He drank a glass of water. 'I'm out of practice for the serious stuff. We only drink wine and spritzers in Venice.'

'It sounds wonderful,' said Bethany. 'I must visit some time.'

'You spent your honeymoon there, didn't you, Peter?' said Marion with unwonted tactlessness, as a result of which Bethany was obliged to telephone the next day and intersperse her thank-yous with judicious enquiries as to Peter's marital status.

He stayed on a few more days, not knowing what to do with himself, wandering about in search of cheap places to eat. Because he felt he must, he went up the Empire State Building, up the Statue of Liberty, and across to Staten Island on the ferry. Staten Island stank of sulphur. He had never felt so lonely in his life.

Bethany rang him one evening, and he had no excuse for refusing to go to dinner with her. 'My city, my invitation,' she said, which was as well, since his money, in spite of a diet of cafeteria food, was running very low.

After dinner, Bethany took him back to her apartment where, with great efficiency, she supplied him with a condom. He did his best to sing for his supper, and managed to do well enough to say, ironically, to himself that he must think of England and not let his fellow countrymen down.

As soon as possible, he sent Bethany some flowers with a card to say thank you, and went home to Venice.

For Giovanni, owner of the Hotel Iris, his wife, Maria, and their family, Christmas dinner was on Christmas Eve. 'I come from the south,' said Giovanni. 'We will be having pike. It is what we have.'

Judy suppressed a shudder. The thought of pike made her feel sick. However, the way it was cooked turned out to be quite delicious.

They all gave each other presents, drank a great deal of wine and listened to the bells clanging stupendously all over the city.

On Christmas Day, all Venice was silent; eerily silent, as it was shrouded in fog. Peter and Judy, with hangovers, took themselves for a long walk, constantly losing their way. Suddenly, Judy sat down on a bench beside the canal.

'I'm pregnant,' she said.

In the hotel, Maria said to Giovanni, 'She is expecting a baby.'

Giovanni asked her if she was sure of this. 'It is her brother she lives with. Surely they *are* brother and sister?'

'Surely, yes. It is someone else. She is a virtuous woman; perhaps she is secretly married, perhaps against her family's wishes.'

★

'Does Larry know about this?' asked Peter. 'I presume it is Larry's.'

'Well, it's certainly no one else's. But no, Larry doesn't know. I suppose, if he comes back, I will tell him. But I've no intention of pursuing him. I can manage by myself.'

Judy as a little girl came back to her brother. She always liked her clothes just so. Her half of the bedroom she shared with Ann was the tidy half. Fastidiously, she pushed Ann's muddle of belongings out of her way and lined up her dolls and teddies on the smooth coverlet of her little bed. Her mother, loving but slapdash as the mother of four children is apt to be, was not allowed to tie her party sash: 'Let me do it. I can manage by myself.'

'Oh, Judy, are you sure? This is a child, not an advertising assignment. How will you support it, without a father? And is this fair to Larry?' It pained him to be reminded of his exclusion by Marion of the fatherhood of his own baby, even though the poor little thing had not been born alive.

'I'll manage,' said Judy stubbornly. 'I'll go back to England and get a job again.'

Peter had started to give the Pizzeros' eldest child, Fabiola, English lessons. She was a bright girl, lively and eager to learn from him, and he was surprised at how much he enjoyed teaching her. At eighteen she had the irresistible energy of youth and was restless and naughty at home, so lessons moved out of the hotel and into the coffee shops which decorated Venice's streets and squares. As they sat huddled in a warm corner and Fabiola giggled away, she learned. And Peter discovered he was enjoying himself. His success with Fabiola made it easy for him to collect a few more students – schoolfellows of hers and a few young men who wanted to get work in England and America. Although the young men were never as much fun as Fabiola, he found the teaching pleasant and easy, and it had the added advantage of being paid for in cash.

His motive for getting this work, apart from the increasing need to make ends meet himself, was the assumption that his sister would need support. He had, however, reckoned without Judy's stubborn streak.

# 14

Laura saw David Nott only from time to time. Occasionally they had a cup of coffee together on a day when he had been court-reporting. Sometimes they had a telephone conversation. She never rang him; she was concerned that his wife might manage to pick up the telephone and be distressed to hear a woman's voice on the line. But she was always elated when he had reason to call her. His second article, the one on 'Second Chances', had been received equally as well as the 'Empty Nest' piece. Readers had responded well to them, as they had to further pieces about women, and he wanted to do more on the subject.

'Not such an empty nest after all,' said Laura, during one such telephone conversation. 'My older daughter is coming home to England soon. She's expecting a baby.'

'She's married?'

'Oh no, I don't think so.' She began to laugh.

'What's funny?' asked David.

'Oh, sorry. No, it's not funny. I mean, I wish she was married, like Ann. But no sooner do I get little J. L. off my hands than another one comes along. Oh well, I'll manage somehow. After all, you manage to do a proper job and look after your wife.'

'I don't do as well as I should,' said David, feeling a wave of the guilt that so frequently assailed him. He felt guilty about the relief it was to get to the newspaper office, to go out interviewing interesting, well, women like Laura Fenby. He felt guilty about his mistress, Susie, as a basically decent man must when he is making use of a woman. He wondered how Laura would react if he told her about Susie. 'So tell me about Judy.' he said. 'What is she going to do?'

'I haven't heard all that much about it yet, but I've told her she must stay here until after the baby is born. Then I think she wants to go back to work and support it herself. Needless to say, her father is horrified, and I must admit I don't much like the idea myself. But she's always been a girl to do things her own way.'

'You're very close to your children. I envy you. I'm so totally out of touch with mine.'

'Does that make your wife unhappy?'

'I don't think so. I don't quite know. I talk about them, of course, but it's hard to tell if she remembers them at all.'

'But she knows you?'

'She's certainly happier when I'm around. In her way, that is. So it must mean she knows me.'

Laura thought about this unexpected new friend she had made, and hoped, with his lonely married life (or more accurately no married life), that he found consolation elsewhere.

Judy came home to the Grange. It was not easy for Laura to know what to do with a daughter, however much she loved her, who was lumberingly pregnant, and about the house.

She took her to see her grandmother. 'I don't remember the wedding,' said Veronica, 'but then, nobody bothers to tell me anything.'

'There wasn't a wedding, Granny,' said Judy.

John was disapproving. Just as he loathed divorce, he also disliked this ghastly modern trend of single parenting. 'Single parenting. Illegitimacy, that's what it used to be, and still is, in my book.'

Judy, although she was determined to have this child, for whom she had already bought chic baby clothes in Italy, and a very grand designer bassinet ('My pram's much nicer than Ann's was,' she said childishly), was bored with the time it took. She resented her lack of control over nature.

To relieve the tedium, Laura invited her to come and sit in court on her bench days. Her mother's involvement in this work was the one thing that really did impress and interest Judy. She usually found herself a seat in a corner of whichever court her mother was sitting in. As her pregnancy advanced, it was necessary to exert considerable self-control in order to sit still. The pressure on her bladder was uncomfortable, and she frequently wanted to go out and find the ladies'.

On the journey home one afternoon Laura was touched as Judy said, 'You know something, Mum. I was bursting to go out for a pee, but I couldn't leave. I was so interested, watching you. You're awfully good at it.'

'Am I? I'm really pleased you think so.'

'It seems to me quite wrong that you don't get paid.'

'Oh well,' Laura replied pacifically, 'that's the way it is. Most of the men are retired, or have reached a stage in their work where they can take the time to sit. And women like me have husbands who support them.'

She could not help but feel rather sad at the thought of the difficult road ahead for Judy, alone. Laura realised that it was not easy for her to understand a daughter so very different from herself.

'Is there anything helpful I can do, while I'm here?' Judy asked.

'Yes, there is, actually. You could go and call on Pamela Bartlett for me. You remember, she and her husband bought Marion and Jeremy's house. I'm afraid I rather let the side down. Dorothy Carew asked me to help her out when her nanny left and she was pregnant with her second baby, and I was too busy. I was in the middle of my training for the bench, you see, but I've never got round to making it up to her or explaining ever since.'

'But surely, anyone would understand that?'

'I didn't say that was what I was doing.'

'Whyever not?' Judy was astonished, and equally astonished by her mother's reply that she had feared she wouldn't succeed and daren't say anything about her venture until after she had been appointed.

Judy readily agreed to go, and added, 'How shall I explain myself? What am I supposed to be, married or what? Or should I be a tragic widow?'

'I think it's better not to try and make up explanations, you'll only get into a muddle. Say nothing. Your decision is your own business and nobody else's, not even mine.'

Fortunately, Pamela Bartlett's questions were of the nature of 'Did you like Italy?' and when was the baby due, followed by the details of her own two births and lavishly illustrated advice on the care one had to take in choosing a nanny.

Judy, while not greatly warming to Pamela, found her very easy company. She had never had quite the same feelings as her sister and brothers for what had once been Marion Clark's wild garden, so she was able to praise the new swimming pool quite genuinely. And she shared Pamela's views on Marion's good taste: 'Amazing, really. Usually when you buy a house, the first thing you have to do is rip everything out and start again. But Mrs Clark's furnishings you couldn't fault. Such a pity she had to leave. Did you know her well?'

'Very well indeed,' said Judy. 'She had no children of her own, and she was lovely to us all when we were little. My favourite treat was when she would let me hold her precious glass vase. I felt so trusted.'

'You must have had a very happy childhood,' said Pamela. 'Swanmere is a wonderful place for children.' They were drinking coffee in the pretty drawing room which had been Marion's. The door was pushed open and a cleanly dressed little boy the same age as J. L. came in with a beaker of juice in his hand. 'This is Toby,' said Pamela. 'Toby, say how do you do to Mrs . . .?'

'Just Judy will do.' Judy took the little hand the child had been taught to hold out. 'How do you do, Toby?'

'Toby, darling, I think you had better drink that juice in the kitchen.'

'Greta said you were in here with a visitor and I wanted to see the visitor.'

'Well, you've seen her now. Off you go.'

'May he stay for a little?' asked Judy. 'I know very

little about children. My one is a bit unexpected, so I have a lot to learn.'

The door opened again, this time to admit a very young German girl holding a baby in her arms and looking a little nervous. '*Toby, komm mit,*' she said. Toby went. On the way out, he stroked the girl's long smooth leg and was just prevented by her from pinching the baby.

Judy continued to observe her mother's magistracy with fascination. But there was one court into which she could not go. The Youth Court was, she learnt, closed to the public and to the press. The only people permitted were the children's parents.

'But,' said Laura, 'the sad thing is that we practically never see a parent.' She had no desire in the world to preach, but she could not help adding, 'Very few of the children have a mother and father living together. Sometimes, if the mother has gone off and the child is with its father, we might see a granny. But if the mother is on her own, she's usually trying to earn money somehow. I learn from the probation officers and the social workers that the mothers genuinely want to do right by their kids, but their lives can seem so hopeless.'

# 15

Peter Fenby, in Venice, tried not to feel lonely. His brief visit to New York had convinced him that his love for Marion Clark had got to be consigned to the past, something about which he had got to pull himself together. His marriage to Deirdre was over and gone, an episode for which he blamed his own weakness. He did not know how to pride himself on having entered that situation as a result of the gentlemanly attitude he had inherited from his father.

Venice was full of pretty women. Occasionally Peter would take one of them to bed. He made love well, and managed to enjoy doing it now on a superficial level.

He had become very fond of Giovanni and Maria, of Fabiola and the children. He hadn't been long in their hotel before Maria, although no longer young, had a new baby. She was philosophical about this: 'Oh well, that's the way with babies. This I didn't need, but God sends. You should have children, Peter.' It was no time to tell her that he had once nearly been a father. Only Judy knew about that. His little dead son was a thing of the past.

He missed Judy. His reserved, understating sister had become someone he was very comfortable with.

Venice was not yet inundated with tourists. The few who came now were not the sort of people who looked to Italy for perpetual sunshine. They were those who just came to Venice because it was a city to see, in its perfection.

One afternoon he was sitting in St Mark's Square, drinking a cup of coffee. 'Pete? How are you? They said at the hotel that you had gone out for a walk, and you might be here.'

'Larry!' said Peter. 'How nice to see you.'

Larry Cunningham sat down. 'I came back,' he said. 'I didn't think I would. Judy was so cool, you know. So I left. But I had taken a great shine to her. And I began to miss her. Would you think she would still want to see me?'

'I don't know,' said Peter.

'I'd like to talk to her.'

'She's not here. She's in England. She's gone home to stay with our parents for the time being.'

'I'm disappointed,' said Larry. 'I had her fixed in my mind as living here, in Venice. Why has she gone back to England?'

Believing he had no right to divulge what Judy had told him in confidence, Peter merely shrugged and said that he supposed there was nothing to keep her here any more. 'I expect she wants to get another job and get back to work. She was used to being a high earner before she came out here.'

When Larry had started making love to Judy, he had seen the affair as an agreeable pastime for both of them, the sort of thing people do when they are away from their own environments. Having married young and, at the time, been passionately in love, he had no intention of falling into that trap ever again. Although his divorce was comparatively recent, the marriage had been a disaster area for years, trailing along towards its dismal death via 'staying together for the sake of the children'. Neither Larry nor his wife was aware that the day they filed for divorce was the happiest day of Martha's and Jack's lives.

While still married, Larry had had two or three affairs, one, incautiously, with a single woman who planned to become the second Mrs Cunningham, a role he had no intention of letting anyone fill, one expensive and acrimonious divorce being, in his opinion, quite enough.

Judy Fenby was a delightful lover, and rather a quiet one, more given to body than verbal language. There were no great declarations of love, but even so Larry began to realise that falling in love was what was happening to him. He decided he was swimming in dangerous waters, which was why he forced himself to quit while he was, in his own words, 'ahead'. Only when it was too late did he discover that not only was he not ahead, but had no wish to be. He pined for this cool, quiet, undemanding woman.

None of this did he tell Peter now, as the two of them sat drinking coffee together. But he knew he could not leave Venice, unless to go to England and find Judy. He stayed close to Peter in the ensuing days, because Peter represented Judy. He was like a dog that clings to its owner's coat in perpetual hope of her return.

Soon Larry was surprised to find himself beginning to value his new friendship with Peter in its own right. His first impression of Peter had been that he was a weaker person than his sister. It was hard to see much in a man who would leave, in these tough days, a perfectly good, if boring, job to live on a teacher's wage in a cheap hotel in Venice.

Larry stayed in much grander digs, a hotel in which he had access to everything that was necessary to run his business back in Chicago. This was a retail store which he had built into a profitable success, and in which he had installed a staff of people trained by him to take his directions from wherever he elected to give them.

Sometimes he would dine with Peter at the Hotel Iris. He enjoyed this very much. Giovanni and Maria usually came to the table, the baby on Maria's lap, and a small, sticky toddler in tow, who would put his paws on Larry's smart trousers. Maria asked him about his children. That he was divorced did not shock her; he was American, after all!

Some evenings Larry would persuade Peter to dine at his expense, always a much grander affair than the spaghetti and omelettes of the Hotel Iris. What they inevitably did, whether dinner was pasta or oysters and steak, was to drink a great deal of wine together. As the night wore on, Larry almost always offered Peter a job.

It shocked but did not offend him that Peter invariably turned him down. 'Nice of you, Larry, but I don't think I'd do. I'm not really a businessman at heart. I was a disappointment to my wife in that respect.'

'And I *am* a businessman at heart. I suppose that had something to do with what went wrong with my marriage – I just wasn't attentive enough to keep my wife happy. Your sister Judy is a very different sort of person. I wish I had her working with me.'

'That's out of the question, right now.' Maybe it was the second bottle that made Peter incautious. 'I should tell you she's expecting a baby.'

Larry was rocked into stone-cold sobriety. 'She's what? Whose is it?'

'I'm pretty certain it's yours.'

'But I thought it was . . . all right. She told me it was safe. Moving to Italy had upset her usual rhythm.'

'Well, I don't know about that, but I can assure you that when she met you, a love affair was not what she was looking for. For all she's so successful, she has very little confidence in herself as a woman.'

Having said that, Peter sat thinking about Judy. He wondered. Ann was the younger of the two sisters. Ann had a child. Was something falling into place? He had been with Judy while she was buying all the smart layette for her own baby. Hers was to have the best. And yet he couldn't believe that she had deliberately become pregnant, even though she was now so determined to go through with it. He was certain that Larry's lovemaking had, at the time, caught her by surprise, and found her unprepared.

Her determination on secrecy was also typical of his sister, who had learnt to have no faith in any relationship.

Into this silence fell Larry's words: 'I am in love with Judy.'

The next day Larry Cunningham walked about Venice, going in and out of shops and wondering whether Judy had bought little clothes for his baby there.

Peter thought quite a lot about Larry. He had got to like the man. He also thought about Judy.

# 16

Mrs Bean's back was, it turned out, rather more than a minor problem. Her sudden squeal of pain on the stairs, while clearing up after J. L.'s uninhibited free fall of vomit, had heralded the onset of a long-term and severe attack of sciatica. 'Oh, I am annoyed, Mrs Fenby,' she said. 'Anything I've ever had before, I've been able to work my way through. I've tried to go on these last few months but now Dr Hallows says it's got to be rest. And just when you've got Judy to look after, as well.'

However, Judy's pregnancy had reached the point where she was filled with the sort of vigour that demands to be let loose in cleaning and tidying. The Grange didn't know itself. She was through it from attic to cellar.

'What's in this chest?' she enquired one morning, while vacuuming the upper landing.

'A few of the things I had for you lot when you were little. I gave the best of them to Mrs Bean, when her Sheila was expecting.'

'These Viyella gowns, may I have them?'

'Of course, if you want them. But you've already bought such lovely things in Italy.'

'These are different. No one has anything like these nowadays.'

88

It's a baby, not a competition, Laura thought but didn't say. She was so glad that Judy had come home to her that she had no intention of saying anything to annoy her. She had been horrified that even Ann, the normally easy-going Ann, had been hurt to snappiness over her own inability to keep J. L. any longer. And Judy had always been inclined to be prickly.

Judy was curious to see J. L. Ann had not been at all well, having recently had an early miscarriage. 'Why don't we have her here for a day or two?' she said. 'Honestly, Mum, I can cope.' The pristine state of the Grange was indeed proof that Judy *could* cope. Laura, who had spent a lot of time on the phone to her suffering daughter, was glad to agree.

'Jude, you look wonderful,' said Ann, who was not looking wonderful at all. She had put on some weight, mostly round the middle. While she had been feeling so poorly and depressed, she had lost her proper appetite, with the result that she had been snacking on cakes and sweets. And exhaustion had deprived her of the vigour which normally kept her quite slim. She had had insufficient exercise, and now felt flabby and shabby. She had never been a great one for caring about clothes, and her hair, which had for too long been stuffed under her white chef's cap, was dull, frizzy and ill-cut. She clambered out of the unwashed car, followed by J. L., sucking an empty Smarties tube.

Ann was overawed by Judy, whose bump of pregnancy was elegantly swathed in expensive folds of Italian couture. Judy was therefore happily restored to her older sister role. In the past, in spite of her professional success, she had, although she would never have admitted it, been diminished by Ann's being the first to marry, and the first to have a baby.

On the second day of Ann's visit, Laura attended a seminar. For once she was able to go off with a clear conscience. There was real joy in seeing her two girls getting on so well, and Judy was amazingly good with little J. L., who was loving the feel of her round, silky tummy. 'You're a very tactile boy,' said Judy.

'Is that naughty?' asked J. L. Told that it was not, he looked mildly disappointed.

'I'll tell you what,' said Judy. 'Let's go over to Cathay Manor and see Granny. It would take it off Mum's back for this week.' In preparation, she washed and cut her younger sister's hair, and made her a present of one of her own blouses. 'Come along, J. L.,' she added. 'Let's smarten you up a bit. We're taking you to see your great-grandmother.'

'Is that naughty?' asked J. L., with renewed hope.

'A bit,' said Judy. 'Get in the car and you will see what you will see.'

Veronica Chadwick was at her usual post in the reception hallway of Cathay Manor. She was seated in the one wing-chair which was easy to get in and out of. It was where she held court and condescended to Miss Fawcett-Smythe.

Veronica could no longer fling one leg over the other. Her feet, which were rather swollen, rested solidly on a footstool which no one else dared to appropriate. 'Who are you?' she enquired, as Judy and Ann approached.

'I'm J. L.,' said J. L.

'Is it Luke?' asked Veronica.

'No, Granny, Luke is J. L.'s uncle,' said Judy. 'I am

Judy, and this is Ann.'

'I'm not senile, I can see who you are,' snapped Veronica. 'It looks,' she said directly to Judy, 'as though you are expecting. So you are married?'

'No, Granny, I am not. I told you that the last time I saw you here.'

'It's all wrong. Ann isn't married, either. That dreadful Len — living together, going to bed in the afternoon, under Laura's roof.'

'Ann is married, Granny. She and Len have been married for a long time.'

'Oh my God, she's really out to lunch, isn't she?' said Ann on the way home. When J. L. had fallen asleep in the back of the car Ann was able to say, 'Judy, do you want to tell me who the father is? Or would you rather not?'

'I'd rather not. He doesn't know anything about it.'

'And you don't want him to?'

'I don't think so. It wasn't that sort of thing between us. He'd just got divorced, so I'm sure he wasn't looking to be tied down again. Typical me, I go for relationships that haven't a hope in hell of lasting, don't I?'

'Was it good? Did you like him? Love him, I really mean.'

'I was getting to. But I'm not going to think about him any more.'


'Pete, how the hell can you live like this?' asked Larry, who was getting rather tired of the Hotel Iris pasta he was obliged to eat, when Peter insisted, as he occasionally did, on standing his whack.

'I manage.' Peter was also now helping out in the hotel, waiting on tables and sitting at the desk in the evenings to greet the non-Italian-speaking guests, mostly back-packing Australians. It meant he got fed and housed for free.

'You really won't take a job with me?'

'No. It's very good of you. But I don't think I would ever belong in America.'

'You could buy for me here. I'll have to go back some time. I wish I could get Judy to go with me.'

Peter was beginning to regret his incautious divulgence of Judy's confidence. She had made it so plain that she intended to manage on her own, that this was to be *her* baby, her responsibility. But Larry had become his friend.

'You could try, I suppose,' he said.

# 17

Ann's visit to the Grange did her good. She became more relaxed and regained her old, sweet demeanour with Laura. 'I do worry about Judy, though,' she said to her mother.

'So do I,' said Laura. 'But she's perfectly capable of making her own decisions. It's none of our business.'

'You really are a remarkable mother. None of our business, you say, when most people's mothers would be interfering like hell, specially with Daddy disapproving as he does.'

'I miss them,' said Judy, after Ann and J. L. had departed. Mostly, she missed J. L.

She was now seven months pregnant. She decided that if, as she had made up her mind she would, she was going to get back to work after the birth of J. L.'s little cousin, she had better start to do something about it. So she telephoned her old boss, Ella Smart.

'Judy, what a surprise! You're back, then.' Ella had not been best pleased when the invaluable Judy had so capriciously quit the company to go off to Venice. She was anxious to have her back, but refrained from gushing about it. Even as they chatted, she was working out how to offer Judy the same job she had had before, at the same salary, not a penny more. A lunch meeting was arranged in London the following day.

Judy was punctual; Judy was always punctual. So she was sitting down at the restaurant table when Ella arrived. It was not until she stood up – Ella was fifteen years older than Judy, and Judy had been well brought up – that Ella observed her condition. Ella was a mother herself. She had two children. She earned a good deal more money than her husband, but she liked him very much, he was a loving father and he didn't in the least mind being the one to take the girls to and from their school.

'How nice to see you, Judy – Oh!' said Ella.

'Oh yes,' said Judy. 'I am, as you can see, pregnant.'

'I didn't know you had got married.'

'I haven't.'

'Do you think that's wise? It's none of my business, but I always think it's better for children to have a father.'

'This one has. It's just that I haven't told him about it.'

Ella had never thought of Judy as eccentric. And of course, lots of people did it this way these days. But it was her opinion that legality made things tidier. She looked at the menu and ordered salad and mineral water. Judy ordered soup and lasagne. She was hungry these days. Ella looked at the mineral water, changed her mind and sent for a bottle of wine.

'Will there be a job for me, if I want to come back?' Judy asked, once they had got to coffee, and she was munching on the chocolates and forming the gold wrappers into little goblets.

'I'd love to have you back.' This was true. Judy's

replacement, hired at a larger salary than Judy had been getting, had not worked out well, and had left, taking a chunk of business with her. 'What about the baby?'

'I gave up my flat when I went to Venice. But I'll find somewhere. If you can pay me the same salary as I was getting, I could get a decent little place, I hope not too far from the office.' Ella was not, at heart, an ungenerous woman, but even so she congratulated herself on not having gone overboard.

'But the baby?'

'When I was in Venice, Peter and I lived at a little hotel. Giovanni and Maria, who owned it, have a large family. Italians are wonderful with babies. I might get their oldest girl to come over as an au pair.'

Ella, insisting upon paying the bill, left the restaurant in an unwonted state of concern. Something was out of place. She had an orderly mind, orderly enough that she had arranged the conception of her own children to fit in with their being born at the quiet time of the year, work-wise.

After lunch, Judy was imbued with the strange sensation that she had forgotten all about London. Though it was not much more than a year since she had left it all to go to Venice with Peter, she had a Rip Van Winkleish feeling. Walking about, she saw no one she knew. Hardly surprising: all her friends had been work friends, and they were all back in their offices and at their desks by now. Regent Street was full of people, not so much hurrying as bumping into each other. Shop façades had changed. I wouldn't be surprised, she thought, to find Liberty's gone. And had Dickins & Jones been so slick and vulgar before she left?

She had to go to Charing Cross to catch the train home. Across Shaftesbury Avenue, Chinatown at least looked the same, with its shuffling Cantonese grannies, old at forty, their triangular eyes vague in their smooth faces, their bent legs shuffling. A crocodile of golden little children was led past her by three teachers, one Chinese, one black, one, the scruffiest, white. She smiled. The children smiled back. Maybe this would be the right environment for the little creature now growing in her womb.

She caught her train. She would not be met at the station. This was Mum's court day, so Judy would take a taxi home. She quite looked forward to getting back to the Grange on her own, and walking about the house in which she had grown up with her brothers and sister.

The only doctor she had seen, since her pregnancy had manifested itself, was Dr Hallows. He was now very old indeed, but he suited her. She had got into this condition in an uncharacteristically unthought-out manner. Dr Hallows was proud of his old-fashionedness. He did not approve of HRT, nor of most of the pills now available to women, not because of any risks attaching to them, of which he knew nothing, but because it was a waste of money, when, in his opinion, women ought to bear their lot and grow old as his own mother had.

Judy made herself a cup of tea, drank it, and went out for a walk. Walks, being natural, were something Dr Hallows recommended quite unreservedly. She crossed the green, and stood for a while by the apparently tranquil pond. Now that the sunshine was strong, the pond had filled up with weed. Two lazy swans drifted across it, stoles of greenery wrapped

96

about their large white façades.

She wondered whether she should look in on Pamela Bartlett, and decided she was too tired. So she sat by the pond, on the seat with the brass plaque in memory of Commander Fortescue, presented by his loving wife. She felt quite drowsy, closed her eyes and remembered pulling Ann out of the pond when they were little, and being cross because Ann, soaking wet, had made a mess of her clean frock. And she remembered how she and Ann had loved going to play at Swanmere Cottage.

Surely Pamela could give a little more of her time and touching to her children? Their father worked all hours, so he couldn't spend much time with them. Well, some children had to do without a father altogether.

At least, thought Judy, sitting on into that sunny evening, I liked the father of my child. Not that Pamela had ever said she didn't like her husband. It was just that there was a cold atmosphere in the house now.

When Larry Cunningham, in trepidation, rang up and asked to speak to Judy, he was surprised to be told that yes, she would really quite like to see him.

# 18

David Nott telephoned Laura Fenby. He had been prevailed upon to take advantage of a day centre where Fiona went for one day every week, so he was alone in the flat. A social worker, young enough to be his daughter, kindly explained it all to him. She was aware that he worked for the local newspaper, an organ that might be helpful to her cause. She hadn't an especially brilliant mind, but she did wish to do well. As usual, the cry was for funding. The young social worker was convinced that more money was all that was needed for all to be well.

David was quite surprised at his need to talk to Laura. He had Susie, after all. Susie was a great comfort, a manifestation of the guilt-free sexual requirements that he enjoyed. Laura Fenby was a different matter.

'David? Hello. Doing another article?' said Laura.

'I'm sort of thinking of this and that. I haven't been in court lately. How's that going?'

'It's all right, but I sometimes get the dreadful feeling that I never do anything properly.' Only last Monday she had caught herself, during a case involving a single mother, before the court for leaving her children alone all night, thinking anxiously of Judy.

Then later, at home, Judy had started to tell her something and her mind had strayed back to the woman in court.

She had pulled herself together in time to learn that what Judy was telling her was of more than somewhat substantial importance. It was that her baby's father, who appeared to be a friend of Peter's, had been in touch, and wished to come and see Judy.

'And have you said yes?' she'd asked.

'I have,' Judy had said, and in her usual way had vouchsafed no more, leaving her mother in the dark as to her feelings for the man.

The distant intimacy of the telephone now released something in Laura. 'You see, when I took on my court work, I thought I was free. I suppose I even thought of needing something to do, and how lucky I was that something as worthwhile and interesting as the bench should come my way. And then Ann needed help with her little boy, and then Judy came home, and although my mother is well looked after at Cathay Manor, I have to go there at least twice a week – she's getting a bit confused now – and my dear Mrs Bean is having to stay away with her back, and now the father's turned up, and wants to come here.'

'Hang on a minute, you're losing me. Whose father has turned up?'

'Judy's baby's father. And we've never met him, and I don't know what John will think about it all, and what on earth shall I give them to eat?' She struggled to regain control of mounting hysteria, pulled herself together, and asked, 'How are things with you? How is your wife?'

'Well, she's at a day centre at the moment. So I'm

doing some household chores. I've got a load of washing in the machine.'

'Can't your daily help do that?'

'She's got too much to do as it is. In fact, I'm not sure if she'll stay.'

Oh my God, thought Laura, that poor man is a million times worse off than I am. To her, after all these years with John, the thought of a man doing the washing and ironing was quite shocking. She was on the verge of offering to go over and do it for him, but had the good sense to realise that this would be an impertinent intrusion. Not only that, but having already poured out her complaints of the pressures on herself, she realised that her friend would never allow himself to add to her load. 'Can you get someone else?' she asked instead.

'I expect so. But I don't mind a few chores, really.' David could not bear for Laura to see him as in any way pathetic. 'I quite like housework. It's exercise, and I can think about writing articles while I do it.'

'I hate to think what would happen to my husband in your situation.'

'Your husband is one man I envy.'

'For my housewifely skills?'

'My poor Fiona had housewifely skills in spades, when she was well. I envy him having a wife to love.'

Laura had not lately felt much interested in sex. She was far too honest to be able to pretend a desire she did not feel. But, hearing John's car come home, she reminded herself that she did love him, always had and always would.

For the first evening in many, John Fenby was received with a welcoming kiss. It gave him great pleasure. Judy, crossing the hall, saw her father put his arm round her mother's waist and give her a hug. 'Judy,' said John, 'be a good girl and get your mother and me a drink, will you?' He led Laura into the sitting room, where they actually had a conversation. Judy handed them their drinks and left them to it. She wondered if Mummy would be telling Daddy about the impending arrival of Larry.

After a while she returned to the sitting room. 'Sorry to burst in on you, but I just wondered, Daddy, if Mummy had told you my news.' It was obvious that she hadn't. Judy took a deep breath. 'Larry is coming to England, to see me.'

'And who is Larry?'

'Larry Cunningham. He's a friend of Peter's and mine, in Venice. Well, rather more than a friend, in my case.' She patted her stomach.

'I see,' said John. 'And is he going to make an honest woman of you?'

'It depends what you mean by an honest woman.' Judy was not going to expose what might be going to happen.

That night John slept with his wife's arms round him.

'So there is a husband after all,' said Veronica to Laura. 'I thought Judy said she wasn't married. I expect it was just to shock me. The young, these days.'

'Did you like Larry?' asked Laura. This was one of Veronica's good days. The arrival, the day before, of Judy and Larry had sharpened her up. Larry was endowed with the formal good manners that are the prerogative of the well-bred American.

'He's American, and a good deal older than Judy, but then Judy's over thirty, so she must take what she can get, mustn't she?'

Larry Cunningham had arrived at the Grange in a car he had rented at the airport. He and Judy had greeted each other with what looked like no more than a handshake. There were no outpourings. Larry had eaten dinner *en famille* at the kitchen table. 'Roast lamb, Mrs Fenby, how very delicious. We always pride ourselves on how to cook beef in America – rare, you know. But this English lamb, not rare, is very good indeed. Thank you. And such a relief not to be eating pasta.'

'Surely it isn't all pasta in Venice? The Italians have so many dishes.'

'Not in the Hotel Iris, where Peter lives. Where I met Judy.' He made no demonstrative move towards Judy. Naturally careful, he merely behaved like a well-mannered visitor. He was not in a turmoil. He was not young. He had been through the heartbreak of young love and its consequent disasters.

The calmness of Larry and Judy had its effect on Laura. There was a slow peacefulness about the evening. Questions were not asked. When it became time to go to bed, Laura left it to Judy to arrange for Larry's comfort. As far as she could tell, they went together up to the bedroom Judy and Ann had shared as little girls.

# 19

'Do you know London at all?' Judy asked Larry politely. In spite of having between them created a future child, they were, now, curiously shy with one another. In fact, contrary to Laura's belief, they had not shared a room in her house. On the upstairs landing Larry had kissed Judy good night and asked her to marry him. She had accepted. In the morning, he invited her to come to London with him to buy a ring.

He was determined that they should stay at the Savoy. He had once stayed at the Ritz with his ex-wife, with whom he had quarrelled most of the time, largely about her bad manners, and on another occasion at the Dorchester with someone else whom he preferred to forget.

'I've never stayed at the Savoy,' said Judy. 'In fact I've never stayed in a hotel in London in my life. When we were little, my mother used to take us to London for Christmas shopping, and they both took us up for pantomimes and the Lord Mayor's Show. But we always went there and back in a day. Dad said he certainly wasn't going to spend his hard-earned money on putting riffraff like us up in a hotel.'

'What's the Lord Mayor's Show?' asked Larry.

'It's a big parade, with horses and floats and things, all through the city.'

'Like Mardi Gras?'

'Not exactly. It's in November, for one thing. We were always afraid there'd be fog and we wouldn't get there.'

Staying at the Savoy was very different from staying at the Grange. 'It won't harm the baby, will it?' asked Larry in bed.

'No. It's well settled in by now.'

'Tenacious, like its daddy.'

They made love slowly but gloriously. Judy had never been so relaxed in her life. Such words as were exchanged were of a moderate nature. Far from being upset that he had had to learn of Judy's pregnancy from her brother, Larry was deeply touched by her courageous independence. She was his first experience of a completely unexploitative woman. Their physical compatibility was enhanced by the steady growth of their liking for each other. 'I'm getting enormous,' said Judy, gazing at him over her large pink façade.

He recollected their affair in Venice. It had not, at first, meant anything more to him than a pleasant encounter. What had then become great for him was, he had thought, not so exciting for Judy, although he could not help but recognise that his lovemaking gave her quiet but undeniable satisfaction. She had not, he realised, had wonderful lovers in the past. She did not squeal or avow, but he became aware that he was doing something right for this woman, so unaccustomed did she seem to be to considerate and affectionate lovemaking. Strange, she was so attractive, and must have had other boyfriends, although she said little about it.

The confidence which had been shattered by the nastiness of his divorce was gently restored to him by Judy. One night, as she slept so quietly beside him, he had whispered to her, 'You are the prettiest thing I ever saw.' She had not answered. She'd simply put a hand on his head.

Now: 'You are indeed very large,' he said. 'And I put on a bit myself, in Italy. All that pasta at the Hotel Iris. We'll both have to go on a diet, once this little person is born. You'd rather have it here in England, I expect. Your family here, and everything.'

'Yes. And there's another thing. My old boss is expecting me to go back to work afterwards.'

'Do you want to do that?'

'I was pretty certain it was what I would do. I hadn't realised that you would be interested.'

Larry burst out laughing. Interested, indeed. He recollected their affair in Venice: she always smiled in her sleep. Her unforgettableness came as a surprise to him.

Judy found that Larry's knowledge of London was confined to the grander hotels and the usual American routes: Harrods with his ex-wife, the Tower and Madame Tussaud's during one visit on which he had been accompanied by his children. Judy's London, of the Soane Museum, Lincoln's Inn Fields, Chinatown, Neal Street, Long Acre, Regent's Park and the Zoo, was all new to him.

'I never did enough with my other children,' he said. 'I was always so busy. I don't think I even took them to New York. This one will be luckier, it will have London *and* New York.'

Returning to the hotel one evening, they had a

message to ring Laura. It transpired that Ella Smart had telephoned the Grange, expecting to find Judy there. 'I just said you were in London, and that I'd get you to call her,' said Laura.

Lunch was arranged at Rules. Feeling slightly guilty, Judy, although not letting on whom she was bringing with her, insisted that this lunch was to be hers.

'Well,' said Ella, as Judy introduced Larry.

Coming straight to the point, Larry shook hands. 'Larry Cunningham, how do you do? And I am, as you might guess, the father of this,' indicating Judy's stomach. He ordered champagne. Ella, wanting to keep her wits about her — she really did need to get Judy back — asked for mineral water. 'I've heard so much about you, it's a great pleasure to meet you,' said Larry. In actual fact he had heard very little about Ella, except that she had been Judy's boss in the past but he was, he flattered himself, quick on his feet.

'Ella has very kindly offered me my job back,' said Judy.

'At a larger salary,' said Ella, much to Judy's surprise. She had not realised the threatening effect of Larry's appearance on the scene.

'I am aware Judy always enjoyed working with you. And, knowing her as I do, she won't be satisfied to do nothing after our baby is born. She's a woman who is suited to work; I think it's how she is happiest. But I'm very much hoping she will work with me. Naturally she won't want to sever her family connections here, and I wouldn't have her do it for anything. But I am going to ask her to make her main home with me in the States. I have a business, retail, in Chicago.'

Ella's interest visibly perked up. Larry might be

removing Judy from her team, but he now glowed in the light of a potential client, and an American client at that.

'Typical Judy,' said Ann to Len. 'You know this baby she's expecting? Only now does she tell me it has a father.'

'They usually do,' said Len. 'Who is it?'

'He's called Larry Cunningham, and he's American. She's staying with him at the Savoy.'

'The wages of sin? That's more than you ever got from me.'

'She'd like to bring him here. He wants to marry her, it seems. And she wants us to meet him.'

Len, who liked Judy, reflected on how very different she was from his own Ann. So smart, yet so insecure and now, it seemed, she needed a second opinion before she would commit herself to trusting her own child's father. He was glad to agree to their visiting. It was in his nature to be kind, and he also felt guilty about having taken so much advantage of Laura in the care of his own baby, J. L. He really had no conception of the pressure of her magistracy, but he did know her as a loving mother-in-law and mother, who minded a great deal about the happiness of her family. In his simple way, Len saw himself as the brother who would demand that this Yank should make an honest woman of Judy.

'When will we get married?' asked Larry. He had liked Len and Ann very much, and had been bowled over by J. L., for whom he had bought a lavish collection of toys from Hamley's.

'Getting in practice for spoiling our one,' he had told Judy, patting her stomach lovingly. 'I didn't do too well by my first family. This is something I'm not going to miss out on.'

J. L. had been equally pleased with Larry; as he had bounced back and forth a good deal between his parents' and grandparents' homes, he had become accustomed to meeting people. So he was friendlily disposed towards this nice big man, who added to his charms by turning up a veritable midsummer Santa Claus.

Even so, Larry was quite glad to be back at the Savoy. Ann and Len's home was not very comfortable. They lived over the restaurant. It was small as yet – a village shop with an upstairs and a back yard with an old stable in it. Plans were already afoot for extending. The room which Larry and Judy had been given had rather a narrow bed, small, worn towels and no bed-side lights. Any money Ann and Len could lay their hands on was ploughed into the restaurant.

Larry liked to read before he slept, a taste shared by Judy. Lying reading, with his arm round her, he said, 'I feel as though we are married already. Is that very dull for you?'

'Not in the least,' said Judy calmly. 'But I think Mummy would like it if I were to be married before the baby is born. Unless you'd rather wait until I can look more presentable.'

They were married in Swanmere. It was not the first time Theodore Carew had married a pregnant bride to a divorced groom, and he had christened so many bastards that he was full of congratulations at their decision. Ann and Len came, with little J. L., who sat on Mrs Bean's lap throughout the service. Luke came, but Mary refused, saying that weddings were affairs she did not go to. Peter sent a piece of non-tourist Venetian glass, which had cost him a lot more than he could afford. Ella Smart came, accompanied by her husband. She was not very fond of him but he was the father of her children, and he was extremely presentable, which mattered in the circumstances. She had every intention of gaining Larry's business for her firm.

All in all, it was a happy day. Dorothy Carew, who prided herself upon being non-judgemental, merely observed, later, to her husband, that 'times change'.

The happy couple stayed on in Swanmere after the wedding. Dr Hallows, her old-fashioned doctor, threw up his hands in horror when Judy suggested that she and Larry would like to go to Venice for a post-wedding trip. 'Fly? At this stage? Complete madness.' Dr Hallows had, as a very young man before the war, flown from Croydon Aerodrome to Paris, an unnerving experience during which the plane had bounced about so much that he had been shot up out of his wicker chair and came down to find himself sitting on the prongs of a silver fork from the luncheon basket, which had made four holes in his backside.

Laura gave a simple lunch. Larry addressed her throughout as Mrs Fenby. 'I call her Mum,' said Len.

'I'm too old for that,' said Larry.

'Then you had better call us Laura and John,' said Laura.

Larry believed that he had never been in a more idyllic spot than Swanmere. So gentle, so tolerant, and so peaceful, a place he would like to live in some day.

'Are you sure,' he asked his new wife, 'that you will like Chicago?'

'I can't wait,' said Judy.

She waited only until after the birth of Laura Ann Cunningham.

## 20

Come September, the Grange was reduced to the occupancy of only Laura and John Fenby. They had both taken a great liking to their new son-in-law, Larry Cunningham. Laura Ann Cunningham, an enchanting baby, had been christened. Luke stood as godfather, although Mary refused to join him in this responsibility. Ann was godmother. Larry stood proxy for his own son and daughter, as a means of beginning to introduce them into the life of their new half-sister. After the christening, the baby was taken to Venice to meet her Uncle Peter, and was made much of by the Hotel Iris family, before the Cunninghams went on to Chicago.

Laura was asked if she missed Judy, Larry and her granddaughter. She made appropriate answers to these enquiries but had to admit to herself that she was, on the whole, elated that Judy had gone to live in the bustle of activity and business that suited her so much better than did life here in Swanmere. She had no qualms for the baby, much loved by both parents, and with a mother who had shown a completely unexpected gift with small children. Clearly, with or without a working mother, little Laura Ann was in for a good time.

While Laura had been busy with both her new life in the courts and her new family members at home, life in Swanmere had carried on. The Bartletts, having settled in to Swanmere Cottage very comfortably, were now taking their place in the life of the village. In spite of the ever-increasing proliferation of executive houses, a sprawling council estate and a new supermarket, Swanmere refused to refer to itself as anything other than the village. Pamela Bartlett was shrewd enough to realise that one went cautiously in this community. She knew far better than to appear to be pushy. Kenneth, on the other hand, spent his weekends taking an interest, and contributing. He had the good fortune to be blessed with a great deal of energy, and little or no sensitivity. He was hail-fel-low-well-met with everyone at the Beaters' Arms, whether they liked it or not. He practised his cricket regularly in the nets, acquired gleaming new whites and gave his strict opinion on those who turned out less elegantly attired. He aimed to be on the parish council, a position he would have little difficulty in attaining, as no one else could be bothered. He also took on Neighbourhood Watch, which meant that his name was down as the contact in case of the arrival in Swanmere of a bogus gasman. As he was never there during the week, Pamela was constantly plagued by calls about suspicious white vans and incontinent dogs.

Pamela was not best pleased about this. She had enough to do, with the two children and a constant succession of departing au pairs. She had taken to going to church. She had in mind the formation of a church nursery school, with the hopeful idea that

Dorothy Carew might persuade Laura Fenby to run the thing. Laura Fenby had four grown-up children, and was a grandmother, famous for caring about her grandchildren.

Dorothy Carew had her own opinion of what Laura's reception of the idea of running a nursery school would be, so made the strategic suggestion that Pamela should have a talk with her herself.

Laura, in her usual way, received Pamela Bartlett kindly. 'I'm sure a nursery school would be a good idea,' she said, 'but it's something I can't possibly do.' She was about to make a lame excuse that she was not qualified, but decided, instead, to brave out the true reason. She explained her magistracy. 'It's much more time-consuming than anyone thinks until they do it.'

Laura tried to explain the hard graft of the background of the job, but what stuck in Pamela's mind was a vision of herself, seated on high in a smart outfit and black stockings, doling out justice and seeing her name in the local paper. There and then she decided she would like to be a magistrate, too. She knew herself to be much more suitable for the job than Laura Fenby, who was only married to a country lawyer whereas she, Pamela, had been personal secretary to a London lawyer before her marriage. And then again, she was years younger than Laura, so therefore much more in touch with today's world. She endowed Granny Fenby with steel-rimmed specs, lavender water and every accoutrement of Victorian old age bar a mob cap and shawl.

'How did you get it?' she asked, her mind now totally divorced from nursery schools and attached to the bench and its future adornment by herself. 'Well, of course,' she went on, 'You know the right people, move in the right circles, don't you?'

Laura was at a loss as to how to answer this. She supposed it was true, but she had never thought of her Swanmere life as being either right or wrong. It was simply where she had lived for more than half her life. She was aware of Kenneth Bartlett's vigorous onslaught on village life. She was also guiltily aware that she hadn't taken much of a liking to Pamela. All the more reason to give her remarks the benefit of the doubt and put them down to ineptitude rather than deliberate offensiveness. 'I don't know,' she said mildly, 'it just seemed to happen.'

Some days later she had a telephone call from Pamela Bartlett. It was an invitation to dinner. 'Just ourselves. I hope it won't bore you, but I thought, well, we don't see enough of you.'

'Dinner with the Bartletts on Friday?' said Laura to John. 'Is that all right with you?'

'I suppose so,' said John without wild enthusiasm. 'It'll save you cooking for a night.' In which gracious frame of mind he accompanied his wife to Swanmere Cottage.

The evening did not get off to a good start. Asked for seven thirty, the Fenbys were punctual. Their host was not. 'Kenneth's late, I'm afraid,' said Pamela. Laura, who had, believing this to be a simple supper for four, merely exchanged her day's gardening trousers for a grey flannel frock, was taken aback by Pamela's outfit of flowing silk trousers and a blouse with high padded shoulders and low cleavage, hung about with gold chains.

In spite of plates of nibbles prominent on the coffee

table, it was evident that no drinks would be poured until their host arrived. Later, John paid Laura a bitter compliment. 'Good God, I can't see you letting our guests sit without a glass in their hands if I hadn't got home.'

During this uneasy, alcohol-free silence, there was the diversion of the door crashing open and the entrance of a smelly and soaking wet child. Pamela seized him, dragged him to the door and yelled through it, 'Irma, where the hell are you?' Eventually, a spotty teenager with a miserable expression on her face came and removed the howling child.

Kenneth bustled in, exuding citified importance. 'Will you,' said Pamela icily, 'give our guests a drink, *please*.' John was given a too-strong gin and tonic, and Laura a too-small and too-sweet sherry.

Curious as to what they were to be given to eat, Laura wondered when Pamela would have had time to create the *Hello!* magazine meal. A long time earlier, was the answer. Dinner, of great elaborateness, had obviously been kept for hours. The avocado pears were brown, and the prawn sauce had gelled glutinously. Some kind of a chicken dish managed to be both dry and greasy at the same time. It was served with rice which had not been nice rice in the first place and was now spectacularly nasty. The pudding was some sort of apple meringue, with apples too sour, meringue too sweet.

Kenneth produced reasonable wines, the drinking of which had to be paid for by listening to an endless dissertation on their provenance.

However, now that this dismally elegant repast was under way, Pamela set out to be a charming hostess, particularly to John.

Getting through post-prandial coffee, Laura did her best with Kenneth. It was easy. 'You play cricket?' she said, and got a plentiful reply.

'Oh darling,' she said to John as they at last were home and making ready for bed. 'I am sorry about that. Poor you, what a bore.'

'Oh, he's dreadful, I admit. But she's all right,' said John.

## 21

In bed, John Fenby felt a need to make love. His wife had brushed her hair, her thick, healthy hair that had bleached with time from pale blonde to a creamy ash. She had lost a bit of weight since she had been so busy with the court and its doings. As a result, the skin on her arms was looser than it once had been, in fact, a little bit wrinkly when her arms were by her side. She had always had that very fine sort of skin that tends to thin. But John's eyesight was not as sharp as heretofore, so he just got into bed and reached out for his spouse, taking her four-child breast in his hand as familiarly and as friendlily as if it had been a favourite pencil on his desk.

Laura was due in court the next day. Before going out to dinner with the Bartletts she had been assembling her mind. She had not thought about making love to her husband. She was taken by surprise.

John, who had been a faithful husband for years, had begun to feel his age. His legal practice, although satisfactory and rewarding, was not prone to excitement. Wills, property and probate had paid for the education of his sons and made up to his daughters, with riding lessons and party dresses, for the rough and tumble of the state education.

Having started out as the youngest partner, he was now the oldest. He had always liked older clients and got on well with them, and now almost all his clients were old, whether he liked them or not. His connection with his children, while affectionate, had been that of a father who regards his young, especially the girls, as being their mother's province.

Pamela Bartlett had come as a surprise, as had her flattering attention. He was quite unaware that she had in mind his possible usefulness. All he knew was that she was tremendously attractive and very charming. That she had bustled the screaming child out of the room and yelled for the au pair, he put down to nervousness at having to receive her guests with an absent host. He also decided that her failure to offer drinks must be because she wasn't allowed, by the overbearing Kenneth, to do so. He had not noticed the nastiness of the food, for wondering whether or not she was wearing a bra under that slinky silk blouse. She was, actually, but a clever one.

Laura was unaware that Pamela Bartlett, in the dark, was transforming her back into the lissom creature she had been before giving birth to four large babies. Although John's ardour surprised Laura – their love-making in recent years had been pleasantly on a level with having something rather nice for dinner – she responded, at first from good manners and then with great enjoyment and giggles. 'Goodness me, whatever next?' she gasped.

'I'll tell you what next,' said John, 'if you would be so kind. That's made me hungry. How would you like to be a dear girl and go down and make me a sandwich?' Even now it did not enter his head that he might be the one to go down and make sandwiches. He was as manly as ever, and had proved that prostate trouble was as yet at bay.

'All right,' said Laura. 'I don't wonder you're hungry.' Coming back upstairs five minutes later with his sandwich, she said, 'That was a foul meal, wasn't it? Our Pamela is no great cook.'

'I suppose you're right. But she's very charming.'

'Is she? I'm not mad about her myself, but if you like her it simplifies matters. We'll have to have them back. Now I really must get some sleep. We've got a full list in the morning, including, you might like to know, a marital rape case.'

Laura had sternly to put out of her mind the unfortunate fact that the marital rapee was not blessed with either good looks or charm. Greasy hair, fat, blotchy cheeks and a voice like a road drill must not be construed as a reason to pity the husband rather than to condemn his act, should it be proved.

As it turned out, the case was absolutely ghastly. The husband, a weedy shrimp who looked more like the beaten than the beater, had a long history of violence, mainly towards his wife. No wonder, thought Laura, that the poor woman no longer bothered to wash her hair; no wonder the comfort of chips and chocolate, coupled with permanent indoor confinement, had wrecked what might once have been girlish skin. The Crown Prosecution Service had brought before the magistrates' court a ghastly saga of burning and kicking. And yet this unfortunate, unattractive female had, whether from some remnant of love or from fear, never actually got rid of the little monster.

It was not within Laura's court's power to deliver

the sentence the husband deserved, so they were obliged to send the case forward to the Crown Court.

After this horror came a case of consoling dullness, respectable in comparison, connected with the theft of a ball of string and a packet of Blu-Tack from W H Smith, after which Laura felt she had earned a cup of coffee and a snack.

She would be sitting again in the afternoon. Sometimes, when this was the agenda, she took the speedy and easy option of going to the canteen. It was frequented by the solicitors so she never lingered, aware that her presence could inhibit their conversation, especially if their clients were not coming into court until later.

With this in mind, today she went down the road to the pub. It was almost empty, so she took her coffee and bun to a table where she could sit and think. The marital rape case had been not only sordid, but also sad. She wondered if that woman had ever loved her husband. Had there been a day, long ago, when she had found him worth washing her hair for? Had she ever spontaneously welcomed him home with a kiss?

Supposing, last night, she had said no to John. When he approached, she had not been in the mood. She had not, in short, felt like it. It had cost her an effort of good manners and kindness to get going. But even if she hadn't enjoyed it, she would have been happy to please John. However, and she chuckled to herself, she jolly well had enjoyed it. Thinking gratefully of how far a cry her own husband was from this morning's man, she stirred her coffee and ate her bun.

'You're smiling,' said a familiar voice.

'David, hello. I didn't see you. Have you just come in? Were you in court this morning?'

'I was. But nothing was making sense to me, so I came away.' He had a gin and tonic in his hand. 'May I get you a drink?'

'No, thank you. I'm in court this afternoon, so I'll stick to coffee.'

'I,' said David, 'am not in court this afternoon. Nor am I going to write a report or do any work of any kind. I am getting drunk. Don't worry about me driving, I shan't. I deluded myself that my car needed servicing, so I left it at the garage where I can't get it until tomorrow.'

'Any particular reason for getting drunk? Is it your birthday?'

'No, it is not my birthday. Yesterday I installed my wife in a nursing home.'

'A nice one, I hope?' said Laura, sounding, to herself, fatuous.

'Well, of course it's a nice one. What do you think it would be?' His voice was three-gin aggressive. 'It was like leaving a crying little child at boarding school. Except that I never did that. All that was Fiona's job. She had to do the betrayal of them that I ducked. Serves me bloody right now that I've had to learn what it feels like to betray her. You wouldn't know. You've never betrayed anyone, have you?'

'My mother thinks I betrayed her.' But this, Laura knew, wouldn't do. She had not betrayed her mother.

'I'm sorry to have intruded,' said David. 'You were looking so happy.'

'I was only smiling at a private thought,' said Laura. She knew she must hurry away. To be late back would be unforgiveable. 'I'm so sorry about your wife,' she said.

On the way back to the court, she drew in deep breaths. The afternoon passed, a petty parade of folly, weakness, failed hopes and unbelievable promises to do better in future.

She wondered, as she left the court, if David Nott would still be in the pub. Maybe he would allow her to drive him home. He was indeed still there, but he seemed remarkably sober.

'Have you been here all this time?' asked Laura. 'You must have been very restrained, if so.'

'Not really. I think I must have drunk myself sober. I like places like this. They change the staff all the time, so no one knows you and you don't have to talk.'

'I find that, as well. I was having a little think myself, when we met earlier.' She had no intention of telling David Nott what it was she had been thinking about. 'If you're worried about your wife, I could drive you to the nursing home. I mean, if you'd like me to.'

'No. I mean, no, thank you. They don't want me to go today. It would only confuse her still further, and upset her for no good purpose.' There was no slur in his voice, but when he stood up he gave a very slight stumble, and grasped the back of his chair. 'You could, however, if you would be so kind,' he said, still speaking with careful clarity, 'drive me home. I am well over the limit.'

It was Laura's first experience of a home that could never have been exactly what one would have chosen, and which had been pared down to make it safe for that poor woman, although even so it had not, in the end, been safe enough. It was centrally heated, with, presumably for safety's sake, not even a gas fire, never mind a proper one. It was not cold, but it was utterly cheerless. Uppermost in her mind was the belief that David ought to have something to eat. But her shyly delivered suggestion met with his asseveration that there were plenty of things in the freezer when he wanted them.

To her surprise, he made a pot of tea. 'Fiona liked tea,' he said. 'It was the one thing she remembered to be particular about. Not tea bags. Proper tea, and warm the pot. I hope they do that in the nursing home. I'm sorry.' Tears coursed down his face. Laura led him to the sofa, sat beside him and took him in her arms. There was no sex in it.

Driving home later, she almost regretted having gone with him to his flat. Until now their communications had enjoyed the detached intimacy of the telephone. Now she feared that they must stop knowing each other at all.

She was very late getting home. 'Where were you?' asked John, who had been worried about her and so was cross.

'I was with someone who needed me, but it's solved. I don't think he needs me any more.'

'Who was it?'

'He's a reporter on the local paper. I've seen him a few times. He interviewed me, and he covers court cases, so I see him there sometimes.'

John pretended to laugh. 'Why the secrecy?' he said.

'No secrecy. I just didn't happen to mention it.'

'Not mention that you were interviewed in the paper? I might have liked to see it, mightn't I?'

'Oh, he didn't use my name. I said he mustn't.

Anyway, I forgot all about it. I just happened to take him home today, because he's very upset about his wife.'

'Has she left him or something?'

'Not deliberately. She's ill, poor soul. He's been looking after her to the best of his ability for a long time. But now he's had to let her go into a nursing home, and he was very distressed about it.'

John told himself there was nothing to worry about in this friendship, nothing in the world to be jealous about. But if so, why the secrecy? With his usual orderliness of mind, he decided to forget the whole thing, or the whole nothing, as it really must be. He succeeded in doing so until three o'clock in the morning, at which hour he woke and fretted until dawn.

# 22

In the early days of his liaison with Susie David Nott had felt, perhaps, a little guilty, but not very. He was not depriving Fiona of anything she wanted. Quite the contrary. Lovemaking had never been to Fiona's taste. In fact, their second child had been installed between them in the bed for almost a year after her birth. She embraced the children kindly but coolly. Him she did not embrace at all.

But now, when he made himself visit her in the nursing home, she clung to him with an ardour he would have welcomed years ago, but which now filled him with sorrow and guilt. He never saw Susie again.

He wondered if he was in love with Laura Fenby. She certainly figured in his restless, frustrated dreams. He was a man of considerable appetite. While still trying to look after his wife, he had been careful not to drink too much. There was enough danger that she might turn on the gas-cooker taps and forget them, or load the dishwasher with dirty clothes, or the washing machine with crockery, without him being witless. These lapses had succeeded her passion for cleanliness, although it still existed in her, as did her detestation of smoking. So he had long ago given up that habit.

After his initial spree at the pub he drank always at

home, and with the car put away in the garage. He was paranoically afraid of losing his driving licence. He must keep his job, he *must* work. The money, he told himself, was needed, not admitting that without the newspaper he would go mad. He bought one pack of cigarettes, and then ten packets. The flat became, he realised, untidy and messy. It was a cheerless prison of walls at best. Its only virtue had been its cleanliness. The cleaner, Alma, departed, on the grounds of being no longer needed, now that poor Mrs Nott was in the home.

David knew he should find out where his children were. The least he could do was to tell them about their mother's illness. With the first whisky of the evening in his hand, he would write (in his head) letters to them. With the second, he would resolve to put investigations in train the next day. With the third, he would turn on the television 'just for the news', and sit in front of it until the late night movie. And so his days passed.

Christmas was coming. But before its advent, Laura decided she must get round to asking the Bartletts back. She thought of chickening out by inviting them to Sunday lunch at the Beaters' Arms. 'Do you think we could do that?' she asked John.

'I don't think so. It would be rather rude, after Pamela took so much trouble to have us.'

An evening *tout seul* with the Bartletts was not an event to which Laura looked forward with delight. For this reason, she rang up the vicarage and invited Theo and Dorothy Carew. It transpired that their daughter Jennifer was at home, so the invitation was extended to include her. Jennifer was a nice girl and had pretty hair.

Although, after her visit to David Nott's flat, Laura had feared that that visit might have concluded their acquaintance, it now occurred to her that to invite him to dinner with her husband and a few friends might well be a good idea.

Jennifer would be the ideal makeweight. Although she was, indeed, seeking matrimony, David would, of course, be quite safe in her hands. Jennifer, as yet eluded by putative bridegrooms, was in constant search of interesting work. She had, Laura had been told, had a poem published, and rather liked the idea of writing. Ergo, David, a journalist on the local paper, might be an encouraging table neighbour. However, poor Jennifer was doomed to sit alone at dinner. David responded to Laura's invitation with a clear, 'No, thank you.' And Laura's attempt to rustle up Luke for the occasion also met with an equally clear, 'No, thank you.'

Throughout dinner, Jennifer remained silent. Being a well-brought-up girl, she had pursued Laura into the kitchen and insisted on helping. This involved carrying in the salad, which wasn't wanted until after the main course, and putting it down on the heatproof mat intended for the boeuf bourguignon, with the result that Laura subsequently burnt her fingers quite badly while trying to shuffle things about.

Tonight Pamela wore black, with a high neck, as befitted a woman with judicial ideas. The time had come for her to close in on John Fenby. 'I've been so interested in hearing so much about the work of a magistrate from Laura,' she began. That she hadn't actually heard anything about it from Laura was neither here nor there.

'Oh yes,' said John. 'I'm afraid she does too much at times, but she enjoys it.'

'But so worthwhile,' gushed Pamela. 'In fact, I'd rather like to do it myself, if I was asked.'

'But your children must be taking up all your time. They're still very young. Laura wouldn't have dreamt of it until ours were grown up.'

Damn and blast Laura, thought Pamela. Aloud she said. 'It's about children I feel so keenly. And actually I do have some legal experience. Furthermore, I believe there really is a need for younger people on the bench.'

'You're quite right.' Laura was honest enough to agree, even though the thought of Pamela Bartlett administering justice impartially was hard to encompass.

Dorothy Carew now put in her oar. 'It's a lovely thought, Pamela, especially helping with children. You'd be marvellous at that, I know. I remember you suggested a nursery school would be a good idea in Swanmere. I'm sure it's something you could organise. Perhaps even in your own lovely home, just a few mornings to help out the working mums. And you have that lovely swimming pool. Such a good idea, teaching the little ones to swim.'

The thought of snotty brats all over her house and garden filled Pamela with horror. 'Safety regulations,' she excused herself, 'and I am not a qualified teacher. I couldn't dare let other people's children near the pool.' She wished she could drown Dorothy in it. If only she could have a few minutes on her own with nice John Fenby! But this was not to be.

After dinner Kenneth buttonholed John, and talked cricket to an extent that almost put John off the game he loved. Dorothy Carew saw Theo beginning to nod, and wheeled him off home. Jennifer, claiming the need for a breath of air before bedtime, strolled over to the Beaters' Arms where, as usual, there was no one interesting to talk to.

Laura loaded the dishwasher and broke one of the good glasses.


To Laura's joy, Peter decided to come home for Christmas, as did Luke and Mary. Judy made long and extravagant telephone calls from Chicago, during which the baby gurgled and Larry, asked to speak, said, 'Merry Christmas,' two or three times.

'Ann and Len are also coming for Christmas,' said Laura to Mrs Bean.

'Nice break for them. Closing the restaurant, are they?'

J. L., dashing through the front door, squealing with excitement heralded their arrival.

'Granny, where's the tree? When can I hang up my stocking? I got you a present, but you can't see it yet.'

Ann and Len followed him, not touching each other. By Boxing Day, it was clear that all was not well.

# 23

It was Veronica who noticed it first. For Christmas was embellished by the presence of Mrs Chadwick, even though, in the run-up to the festivities, Laura had almost forgotten her mother.

Veronica seldom telephoned. In her book, it was other people's duty to keep in touch with her.

When the telephone rang and her mother's quavering voice said, 'Hello, hello?' Laura's immediate reaction was to fear she was ill.

'No, I am not ill. I am not well but then I never am these days. And how are *you*? I haven't heard from you for a long time.' It was, Laura guiltily realised, almost a week since she had been to Cathay Manor.

'Fine, Mummy, thank you.'

'I'm glad to hear it. Are you going away for Christmas? I thought you must be away, since I hadn't heard a word.'

'No. We're not going away. Peter's coming, and Ann and Len and J. L. Luke and Mary will be here, too, but Judy and Larry can't get over until later in the new year.'

'And me? Had you thought about me?'

'Of course I had. I thought you'd rather be at Cathay Manor, with your friends. Would you like it if we all came over on Christmas morning?'

'Did it not occur to you that I might prefer to be with my own family, and not alone amongst strangers?'

'Of course, Mummy. How silly of me. I just thought you'd be more comfortable there, but of course you must come to us. If you're sure you won't find it too noisy.'

'I don't mind that. It's quiet enough here, too quiet. Deathly quiet, actually.' Laura, as was intended, was guilt-ridden. 'I'll only come for the day,' continued Veronica. 'You can take me home in the evening, I don't want to be a trouble.' Thus it was that she was installed at the Grange for four days.

It was Peter who drove over, in Laura's car, to pick Granny up from Cathay Manor. 'I take it,' said Veronica on the way, 'that Deirdre is at the house?'

'No, I'm on my own,' said Peter. 'I've just come over from Venice.'

'Surely you haven't left her alone there over Christmas? Poor girl, I thought it was only when one was old one had to face being alone.'

'Deirdre does not live with me in Venice. Granny, we are divorced.'

'You think I don't remember things,' said Veronica testily. 'Of course I know you are divorced. You young people, you don't even try. I liked Deirdre very much. You should have had children.'

Veronica's arrival was made easier by the bossy interference of J. L., who wished to know who this old lady was. Laura, looking on at this meeting, reflected that early youth and old age had similarities in their approach to life. 'Have you brought me a present?' asked J. L. He had not forgotten the lavish generosity of Larry and Aunt Judy, so was ever-hopeful.

'Have you been a good boy?' asked Veronica. 'If so, we'll see.' The first part of her visit passed off well, in the company of J. L. Veronica had always been at her best in the presence of men of any age. But she had never liked Len. She had always regarded him as common and now, in her opinion, he was looking furtive.

Len was feeling furtive. He had, really, a very simple attitude to life. He liked cooking, moderate imbibing of wine and bonking. His lovely Ann had come his way, and made him happy. J. L. was a dear boy. Then another baby had been on the way, and there was plenty of room in his heart to welcome it. But Ann had miscarried. She did not seem, in the words of his own mother, to have picked up very quickly after that loss. In other words, she had gone off sex. Of course as a modern man he understood that intercourse was painful for her, after all that she had been through. But she hadn't seemed to get over it. And he really did need the comfort of sex. He had got it with a nineteen-year-old girl, Bella, who helped out at the restaurant.

This peccadillo might have remained just that, and soon been forgotten, but the girl not only took him seriously but also fell in love with him. He had run her home one night when her own car had broken down. As luck would have it, it was a night when her parents were away. The whole thing was pathetically obvious. Yes, he *would* like to come in for a coffee. And yes, he *would* wait a minute while she slipped into something loose. The something loose became very loose indeed, and slipped off with the greatest of ease.

Too late, Len discovered that Bella was a virgin. After the moment of grunting relief had passed, he was filled with guilt and shame. When he got home, Ann was walking about with J. L. in her arms. He had had a bad dream and woken up crying. She was too tired to notice how long Len had been away.

Len was too nice and too sensible to assuage his guilt by confessing to Ann. After a day or two, he was almost able to pretend to himself that the whole thing had never happened.

Bella, however, had not forgotten, and did not wish to. In the ensuing couple of weeks she seized every opportunity of getting Len when he was alone, and pouring out her avowals of love. Len, out of kindness and weakness, made love to her twice more and then told her it was all over.

'Look,' he said abruptly, 'this has got to stop. I'm sorry about it, I hadn't realised before that it was going to be the first time for you. But even so . . .'

'I love you,' she wailed.

'You don't really. You'll find someone much better than me, someone your own age, a pretty girl like you. You don't want to waste your time on a married man.'

Alas, she did. Poor Bella was even something of a romantic. So much so that she convinced herself that Len's marriage was only a working arrangement, on account of the restaurant.

In all the years they had been together Ann had believed, with reason, that Len wanted no other woman but her. She honestly had not realised what her temporary period of frigidity was doing to him. So it came as a heart-breaking shock when she was approached by Bella and informed that her husband was not in love with her, and probably never had been. 'Oh well, I know, probably at first he was. But he isn't now.'

'How,' asked Ann, as calmly as she could, 'do you know this?'

'Because he's in love with me. He's trying to be loyal to you, but he loves me.'

'And what makes you think that?'

'I don't *think* it. I know it. He makes love to me whenever he can get away from you. He probably hasn't asked you yet, himself, but I can tell you that divorce is the only answer. Naturally, I expect you'll get custody of the little boy.' She didn't even know J. L.'s name, but that did not stop her from adding, 'But I'll be kind to him when he's with us.'

By Christmas time the trouble was not quite over. Ann had tried to forgive. She was normally a rational, fair-minded woman, but her heart was sore.

What made matters worse was her discovery that all this had been going on just as she was beginning to feel a bit better physically, and had been rather hoping for a cuddle. Bella's fantasy had a devastating effect.

Bella had blonde hair, though Ann couldn't help wondering if, out of sight, it matched. Ann had been herself a pretty young blonde when Len had fallen in love with her. Now she felt drab and shabby, and very sorry for herself.

She had done everything she could to help Len build up the restaurant, even to the extent of handing little J. L., the child she loved, largely over to her mother. She had made puddings and pies, even when she was feeling sick, and had unloaded vanloads of heavy produce. Anything, in fact, to save expenditure on extra staff. And then Len had brought in bloody Bella to wait on tables, which she did not do very well, and on his cock, which she seemed to have done very well indeed.

'It's a bit of a classic, isn't it?' said Ann bitterly, 'the new model? Wear out the old one, and get a younger one to replace it.'

'I don't want her,' said Len pathetically.

'You should have thought of that sooner, shouldn't you, you stupid prick?' This was said as Ann threw Len's clothes into one suitcase, and her own and J. L.'s into another.

As her Christmas guests arrived, Laura got everyone installed to the best of her ability. Mrs Bean came in to help, but Laura was perpetually worried that her back might snap under the strain of mattresses and blankets, so she made up all the beds herself. Luke and Mary made things slightly easier by settling happily into the Beaters' Arms to both Laura and Mary's satisfaction. Much as Laura adored her younger son, the thought of seven visitors in constant residence did not appeal. Mary, for her part, loved Luke's family but preferred the small degree of privacy the Beaters' Arms provided. Luke, being Luke, was pretty much happy anywhere as long as he got to spend time with his lovely, irresistible girlfriend.

Laura put Ann and Len in the double-bedded guest room, in the fond belief that the loving couple must not be separated. She was glad that they had decided to close the restaurant for a few days. They both looked washed out, and she vowed that on this occasion she would allow neither of them to do a thing in the kitchen, and spent days slaving over mince pies, bread sauce and brandy butter.

J. L. was to be in the top room, to which he had earlier become accustomed. Veronica was given the girls' room. 'Rather far from the bathroom,' said Veronica. 'You really should install a second bathroom. Goodness knows, you can afford it.' Veronica was always convinced that everyone other than herself could afford everything. 'You haven't even put in a shower. At least I have a shower en suite at Cathay Manor.'

'That's great,' said Laura. 'How nice.'

'It's never hot enough, but one has to make the best of things when one is old and unwanted.' Veronica's talent was unquenchable.

On Christmas Day, J. L. got, from his great-grandmother, the gift of a one-pound coin, which he did not appreciate.

Miss Fawcett-Smythe had sent, via Veronica, a potted hydrangea. 'Poor old thing,' said Veronica.

On Boxing Day she informed Laura that there was 'something wrong there' in reference to Ann and Len. 'Poor child, fancy marrying that awful young man.'

At last it was time for Peter to drive his grandmother back to Cathay Manor. There, a bit of a disaster had taken place. They were suddenly short-staffed. One of the employees had broken a leg skiing. She was, Laura recollected, when Peter gave her the news, a particularly kind girl who had endured more from Mrs Chadwick than duty demanded.

'Poor girl,' said Laura. 'Was Granny upset about it?'

'Very,' said Peter. 'She wasn't sure if her bed was properly aired. She was furious. A maid aping her betters, is what she said. And added that of course she would break a leg. How could that kind of girl know how to ski?'

Forbidden by Laura to lift a finger, Ann and Len, for

whom wooden spoons and pudding basins might have had a therapeutic effect, were bored and tense. They tried desperately to keep their troubles to themselves. As a result, they quarrelled at night in whispers and icy silences. Ann's poor heart wanted a loving embrace, but any attempt by Len was met with an abrupt move to the furthest side of the bed. When J. L. came in to them in the mornings, he found himself with a lovely amount of space to play with his toys. For the first time in his life, he didn't have to push Daddy out of the way to get a hug from Mummy.

## 24

This Christmas was the first time Peter had gone back to Swanmere since he had taken up residence in Venice. Upon hearing the news, Fabiola sulked loudly; she considered her lessons as entertainment rather than as work, and was annoyed at the idea of being deprived of her playmate for a while. Maria and Giovanni, however, were more equable. 'Going home, how nice,' they had said.

'Not exactly home any more,' Peter replied.

'But of course it is. Your mama, your papa, your family.'

'Of course,' said Peter.

This Italian family, which had so unquestioningly made him one of themselves, actually knew very little about his past. They had a day-by-day talent, having earned their living for so long as owners of a modest hotel, for letting life come and go, and not messing things up by making extraneous enquiries to which the answers would be unconstructive. They knew that Peter was divorced, a state contrary to their own beliefs. Maria had a quick temper, and would hit Giovanni on the head with a frying pan now and then. It was, for her, a much simpler way of dealing with the masculine silliness of which she had learnt at her mother's knee than wasting time on analytical words, which did not come readily to her lips.

They were initially worried that Peter might be homosexual – there was far too much of that in Venice these days. But Peter had been married, so that settled that question. And now his sister Judy was married as well, with a bambina, a dear little girl who had been passed round the tables when Judy and Larry had brought her out to see Uncle Peter.

Having promised to come to Swanmere for Christmas, Peter was filled with dread. He feared his memories of Marion, the one woman he had so desperately loved. But her presence had been, he soon found, completely erased by the Bartletts. The inside of the house was as impeccable as it had been, but the wild garden was gone, replaced by a swimming pool, cautiously surrounded by safety fences, and now under cover for the winter. And Pamela Bartlett, although some people in Swanmere said how nice it was that she ran the house as beautifully as Marion Clark had done, was, emphatically, not Marion.

In a different way from that of his grandmother, Peter could see that all was not well between Ann and Len.

Curiously enough, Veronica's malevolent presence was something of a help to him. For one thing, he was drawn into protection of his mother. For another, Veronica's vulgar awfulness was actually funny. He found himself laughing aloud as he drove home after hearing her strictures, at Cathay Manor, on the poor girl who had had the skiing accident. She had added to the subject with the declaration that, in her day, people had known their places.

He got on very well with little J. L. 'Have you got me a present?' asked the boy.

Unconsciously echoing Veronica, Peter enquired if he had been a good boy. He had, under Maria's guidance, bought a Venetian toy for the child.

In answer to Uncle Peter's question, J. L. replied, 'That lady asked me that.'

'That lady is your great-grandmother,' said Peter. He had brought more Venetian glass for his mother, and a silk scarf for his grandmother. 'Suitable for an old woman,' she said, glaring balefully at the graceful glass. 'Oh well, quite right. There's no point in wasting your money on anything like that for me. I've nowhere to put it, and the maids would only break it.'

From her mother Laura received two very small towels, which Veronica had got mail-order, and which, when washed, dyed all John's underwear bright Ribena-colour. John got a bottle of indifferent wine. Miss Fawcett-Smythe's potted hydrangea was given to Ann and Len. 'I expect,' said Veronica to Len, 'that you usually put those dreadful dried flowers on the tables. This will make a difference.'

During her mother's visit Laura, driven mad by four days of it, dared not fly at her, which might have been a good idea. Instead she bit John's head off, which hurt his feelings considerably.

Peter, aware of the tension between Ann and Len, spent a lot of his time distracting J. L. Living with Giovanni and Maria had taught him to be unselfconscious and tactile with little children, so he had no inhibitions about cuddling and petting the little boy.

Ann, he noticed, seemed to have no appetite. Laura also noticed this, and was made fearful by it. She was not easily convinced by psychological babble, but she had, through her court work, become aware of anorexia. Veronica merely sniffed and said, 'Slimming. They all do it. Fortunately, I'm one of those lucky people who can eat anything and never put on an ounce.'

The only light relief over the festive season had been the presence of Luke. Although aware of the tensions hovering over the Grange, he had been his usual irrepressible self, turning up with weird and wonderful presents for everyone which were designed, as always, mainly for Luke's own entertainment. His favourite this year had clearly been the Scalextric for J. L., which the little boy had hardly been allowed to get near. His enthusiasm was infectious, however, and at times he had nearly broken through the unease which kept Laura, Peter and Ann from enjoying Christmas. Even Veronica occasionally unbent before him.

As Peter watched Mary watching Luke, a slightly reproving yet hugely indulgent smile on her face, he was relieved to see at least one of his family happy. His parents worried him, but he could only hope that things would come out all right in the end. After Christmas he could see only that his father wanted to have his mother to himself, and so he was glad to get back to Venice.

Once home at the Hotel Iris, he was gladder still. The little ones ran at him and anointed his trousers with the English chocolate he had brought for them. Franco, the seventeen-year-old boy who had never left Italy, regarded him as a sophisticate *par excellence* and wanted to know all about England, or 'London' as he called it.

And Fabiola hugged him in the same simple way as did her parents and the little ones.

'I'm sorry,' said Peter, 'I didn't bring you any chocolate.'

'Oh Peter, why no? I like the chocolate, too.'

'I thought you would be slimming.'

'I am too fat?' She was nothing of the kind. She was very pretty indeed.

'Oh, just that people in England always slim. My sister Ann is slimming.'

'*Poverina*,' said Fabiola.

Although she was sadly aware that all was not well between Ann and Len, Laura had decided against asking questions. She felt hopeful that it was just something that would blow over, one of those things that irk after the first few years together. She hadn't forgotten that period in her own life, when waves of resentment blew over her. It was a time when John had seemed incredibly selfish, when she had sole care of two babies, and all he seemed to notice about it were the toys left for him to fall over.

Looking back, she realised what a very good thing it was that she had had no one to confide in at the time. And now she believed that getting a later-to-be-regretted confidence out of Ann would be a poor idea.

She was very glad to be back in court once more. At last the piles of sheets and towels were washed, and she had managed to get her own plain blouses laundered and ironed and ready to wear, so as to be presentably suited. The festive season had had its usual effect, the result of which was an ample number of driving offences, physical assaults and burglaries. At least it was a relief that these had to be dealt with by the head and not the heart.

She looked down from the bench, wondering if David Nott would be in the press seats. He wasn't. She hoped he was all right.

## 25

David Nott sat in the uncomfortable chair beside his hospital bed. He had just been lectured by a doctor who looked to be about eighteen years old. 'You smoke? And you drink?'

There had been a packet of cigarettes in his pocket when he was brought in, suffering from pneumonia. He had also been very slightly drunk at the time.

He had actually spent Christmas Day in a state of total sobriety. He had been absolutely determined to bring Fiona home for the occasion. The matron at the nursing home had advised against it. She was in charge, and the nursing home was fortunate to have her, trained in the old school as she had been. She would have no truck with modern familiarities. Patients were called Mr, Mrs, or, with luck, Sir or Lady. And she was addressed as Matron, and woe betide anyone who transgressed upon that.

'Of course, Mr Nott, you must do whatever you prefer. But she won't know the difference.'

'She knows me,' said David.

Matron kept her counsel. Sometimes Mrs Nott referred to 'my husband', sometimes she didn't.

Christmas morning saw Matron on duty. She herself dressed Mrs Nott cleanly and neatly, and added a warm cardigan. The nursing home was well heated, and she did not trust this distrait husband to see that his own place was adequate in that respect.

For Christmas, David bought a little tree at Woolworth's. He couldn't think what gifts to give Fiona, and ended up by adding to her confusion by putting out packages allegedly addressed by the children. He bought a ready-cooked chicken, a packet of Smash potato, and a Marks & Spencer pudding.

On Christmas Eve he sat with the last whisky he was to have for the next twenty-four hours, and fantasised about Laura Fenby's Christmas. Bleakly trying to make the day nice for Fiona, he imagined the Fenby household. Sons and daughters come home, and a little grandchild, being cuddled by Laura as she had once cuddled her own babies.

When Fiona arrived home on Christmas Day, she looked in puzzlement at the phoney presents. At last she said, 'Do you remember the children?'

'Oh yes,' said David, 'of course.'

'I thought you had forgotten them,' said Fiona, surprisingly.

David was at a loss. 'They are both far away,' he said.

'Both? That's two? I thought there were more.'

He put the crackers on the table and served the food. Fiona ate, vaguely but obediently. He held a glass of pineapple juice to her lips and wiped the drips off her chin. Poor Fiona, she had never been able to bear sticky hands, never mind a sticky face. He helped her to pull a cracker. They were expensive crackers, and Fiona got a pretend diamond brooch, which she wrapped up in a scrap of the cracker paper.

'Why,' he asked, 'do elephants paint the bottoms of

their feet yellow?' Fiona looked blank, as well she might. 'So that they won't be seen if they land upside down in a bowl of custard,' he read out. He thought she might ask why elephants would fall into a bowl of custard. But she said nothing. She had already forgotten the cracker riddle.

He sat through the interminable afternoon, nodding off in front of the television. Fiona nodded off too, but laughed indiscriminately at everything that appeared, including a plea for aid for the starving children of Central Africa.

At last it was time to take her back to the nursing home. As Matron was short-handed over the holiday, he assisted her in getting his wife into bed. The sight of her sagging body and wasted arms embarrassed him as much as if they had been those of a total stranger.

Having seen her patient tucked up, Matron escorted him to her office for a cup of tea and a slice of cake. 'I expect you'd rather have a whisky,' she said kindly.

'I would indeed, but I have to drive home, so tea's best.'

'Very sensible. But I advise a whisky when you get home. This is not easy for you. In many ways, it's harder on you than on her. She's usually quite happy, you know. You would think our routine very rigid and boring but I assure you, it's right for her. People with this condition mustn't be flustered.'

'How long will she live?' asked David, with sudden abruptness.

'Oh, she could live a good long time. She's quite well in herself, you see, so we can be hopeful of that.'

David was not the only one who fantasised about other people's lives. Matron imagined, or chose to imagine, that the stricken Mrs Nott had previously had a long and loving marriage with this nice, tired man.

David put the car safely away. Once in the flat, he got out the whisky bottle. 'Matron's orders,' he said aloud, and added, 'Here's to Matron.'

He wondered why he had refused Laura's invitation to dinner before Christmas. It would have been sensible and level-headed to meet her husband socially. She had put her arms round him the day he had been so miserable and she had driven him home, but only as she would have put them round a distressed child.

He had no idea that Laura had been happy to return to the order of her job in the court. He only knew that he was glad, once the endless double whammy of Christmas and New Year was over, to be back at work on the newspaper. He now had his own byline. Not only were his court reports in demand, but he had also turned in many other good pieces. Now that he had to drive all over the county on stories, he manfully refrained from drinking even so much as a beer while working. This meant he also failed to eat. Many a day went by with no more than a packet of peppermints being swallowed, accompanied by several cigarettes. But when he got home at night, he allowed himself a 'couple' of whiskies before bed.

Inevitably, he caught a cold. Everyone on the paper had colds; everyone claimed to be the illest. David said firmly: only a cold, everyone gets colds at this time of year, let's not fuss. Then came the night when pains in his chest and sides became so severe that he thought he must be having a heart attack. With drunken logic, he decided that he had got to survive. He had got to work, he had got to support Fiona. There was no alternative but to phone the doctor.

The doctor, whose patient the poor chap's wife had been until she went into the nursing home, came round straight away although it was eleven o'clock at night. Seeing the whisky bottle, he merely said, 'Have you had a nip of that?'

'Yes,' said David. 'Would it bring on a heart attack?'

'Well, if it would, it hasn't. You haven't had a heart attack. What you've got is pneumonia. Have you been coughing much?'

'I suppose so. If it's only pneumonia, can't you just give me something for it?'

'Hospital's the best idea. Just a day or two, that's all you'll need, and then you'll be as right as rain again.'

Sitting in his hospital chair, David wondered why he had not the least desire for either a cigarette or a drink. The nurses were particularly kind to him. He was undemanding and courteous, and the only patient in the ward who did not complain about the food. He ate very little, his stomach was out of practice, but what he did eat he forked up like a good child.

By the time David Nott had been a week in the hospital, the young doctor was convinced he had made a convert. This was one patient who did not nip outside and come back reeking of cigarette smoke. The doctor was neither as young as he looked, nor quite as unwise. He had dealt with many habitual drunkards, but he still did not understand the likes of David Nott, whose use of these props was not an indulgence but a means of keeping going.

★

Laura Fenby did not know that David Nott was ill. There was no reason why she should. They were not close. She was busy enough surviving January.

As the year gave way to February, John Fenby found himself confused. He knew the workings and the vicissitudes of the law perfectly well. But he had not, as a husband, taken in how much his wife's work would deprive him of her attention. Proud as he was of her becoming a magistrate, it was not possible for him to equate her with those other men and women who were on the bench.

He was incapable of separating his attitude. His wife, who had always done everything at home, was now neglecting him.

But Pamela Bartlett, who still had her magisterial ambitions in mind, did not neglect him.

# 26

Pamela Bartlett was in the mould of women who do well by having clever bodies and faces, and who come to believe that they have brains to match.

She had held off marriage until the right moment, which came with Kenneth Bartlett. She had endured a good deal along the way. As secretary in a London law firm, no one ever, for one moment, suggested she should be anything more than that. She did, however, get taken out to many a restaurant and many a theatre. Having a wonderful figure, a tall, well-proportioned size 12, it was no problem for her to dress well without spending much money. She knew how to make a plain black or white shirt look very sexy indeed, and she had been given, by admirers, one or two good pieces of jewellery. Quite often, standing about in foyers, she would be taken for someone, such as a model or an actress. Kenneth, ambitious but not yet quite there, took her for such.

She had every right to Swanmere Cottage, the lovely house and garden that belied its humble name. She had earned it the hard way. She did not dislike her children; they were part of the deal. The details of their requirements were intensely boring, and sometimes almost sapped the energy with which nature had endowed her.

It was the bubbling nature of her energy which had first attracted Kenneth: that and her outstandingly pert breasts. Fairly thick himself, outside of his one talent, which was that of making money, he had picked this plum off the tree.

Pamela, by this time, was sufficiently sexually adept to give Kenneth what he needed. It wasn't too much, in actual fact. Although fairly frequent in his requirements, their fulfilment never took very long. The computer on his desk got more foreplay than his wife.

Buying Swanmere Cottage was something about which the Bartletts were in total agreement. They were by now pretty well off, but even so it was satisfactory that a property in Swanmere cost less for more than anywhere in Surrey. And in real-estate terms, the pretty village was advancing all the time.

It also now began to seem that the choice of Swanmere offered advancement to Pamela, who was beginning to believe that she had given up a great career for Kenneth and the children.

She refused to be put off by John Fenby's initial lack of enthusiasm for the idea of her becoming a magistrate. That Laura had not done it until after her children were grown up was neither here nor there. She, Pamela, was a very different woman. A skilled organiser, she had no time for muddle, and had fired three au pairs to prove it. Even with all the work to do herself, her house was still impeccable.

She pursued John Fenby at every opportunity. John was actually somewhat discomfited by this attention. He found overtly sexy women embarrassing. The very fact that he had once made love to his wife while gazing, in his imagination, down the front of Pamela's blouse, was something he preferred to forget.

In order to facilitate her approach to John, Pamela was obliged to cultivate Laura. Having found yet another au pair, she left the children with the girl one morning and called at the Grange. The children didn't mind being left. They were used to a variety of girls and her son was adept at wheedling extra biscuits and chocolate out of these soft touches.

Pamela found Laura dressed in her outdoor coat, car keys in her hand. 'Oh, Laura, you're just going out. Don't let me disturb you. I can come another time.'

'I'm so sorry,' said Laura, ever the apologiser, 'but I'm just on my way to see my mother. I promised her I'd come this morning, and she gets dreadfully upset if I don't arrive when I've promised.' She was not displeased, although a little surprised, when Pamela proposed joining her in the visit. Any diversion was a relief with Mummy.

Unfortunately, Veronica took an instant dislike to Pamela. Laura introduced her, saying, 'I don't think you've met Pamela Bartlett, Mummy.'

'No,' said Veronica.

Laura burbled on, 'She and her husband, Kenneth, bought Swanmere Cottage when the Clarks went to America. Kenneth and Pamela have two children, you know, and they love it there, don't you, Pamela?'

'Oh, absolutely,' said Pamela.

'I used to go there frequently in Marion Clark's day. I was very fond of her,' said Veronica.

'I'm sure. She had wonderful taste. I loved the house the moment I saw it. She had decorated it so beautifully. The only thing we had to do was to clear out that wilderness in the garden and put in the swimming pool.'

'A swimming pool, how very vulgar,' said Veronica in what she pretended was an aside.

'It was for our children,' said Pamela, annoyed to find herself on the defensive. 'Poor Mrs Clark didn't have any children, did she?'

'Children aren't everything,' said Veronica, 'My daughter had four. A terrible tie. She gave herself over to them entirely, to the exclusion of everything else.'

Laura remained silent. She could see how much her mother was disliking poor Pamela, and yet felt incapable of cutting in, even in the defence of her own young. As for defending herself, she had long learnt to save her breath.

'You have two?' continued Veronica interrogatively. 'Perhaps it's wiser not to have any more. Such an expense, these days.'

'So true,' said Pamela. She added, 'In any case, I'm thinking of resuming my career. Well, perhaps not exactly resuming, it's rather a long time ago now. But I do hope to put my previous experience to good use. I'm thinking of offering myself as a magistrate.'

'A magistrate? Good heavens!' Veronica's cattiness was now reaching the all-embracing stage. 'I would have thought there were enough of them already. Every idiot woman in the world seems to be a magistrate these days. In my day, we left that sort of thing to our husbands. For my part, running my home and bringing up my daughter was my job, as I saw it.'

At last it was time for Laura to kiss her mother goodbye, and to swoop in in time to prevent Pamela (who was very much in the mwah-mwah mould) from committing the solecism of trying to do the same thing.

'Your mother,' said Pamela resolutely, on the way home, 'is wonderful for her age, isn't she? And you are so good to her. You and John must dine with us again soon.'

Fortunately for Pamela, she had an opportunity of furthering her acquaintance with John Fenby without actually including Laura. When they had put in the swimming pool Kenneth, with sublime if not actually purposeful disregard of the neighbouring houses, had had it surrounded by leylandii. These were already blocking the light from the garden of a very small nearby house, occupied by an elderly widower whose joy in life was his sunny garden, and who had previously been able to look across at the rambling wilderness that had preceded the pool and its aggressive hedge.

He had tried to talk to Kenneth about it, but had been rapidly snubbed. As a result he had asked advice of John Fenby. 'Let me,' said John, knowing the old gentleman to be very short of money, 'see what I can do in a private way.'

He asked Pamela to come to his office for a chat, in the hope of persuading her to persuade Kenneth that the trees would be thicker and more attractive if pruned right down. Mid-week, mid-morning, was his plan.

Pamela arrived late. Her concept of herself as organised and professional-minded did not extend to punctuality. She swept in, in a haze of Nina Ricci and apologies. 'So sorry to be late. It's just as you said, John, children!' She had given the au pair a bollocking that morning, as a result of which the unfortunate girl had been reduced to tears, and so had the children.

John came to the point as quickly as he could. Pamela was charming and co-operative. 'Of course I'll see to it, John. I'm sure Kenneth didn't want to cause trouble. He just doesn't know how things grow. I'll have them cut right back, and he won't even notice. Neighbourliness is *so* important, isn't it?' She went on about neighbourliness and her own virtues in that respect for so long that suddenly it was almost one o'clock and John was obliged to invite her to join him for lunch.

Laura had been in court all morning. Unless there was a continuation in the afternoon, she usually went straight home. But on this occasion she needed to go to Marks & Spencer's. So for once she went from the court, which was well outside the town, down into the centre.

Having done her shopping, she wondered if John would be having his lunch at the Crown and Orb. She knew he often did. When sitting on the bench she seldom spent time over lunch, preferring a quick coffee and a snack, in view of the need for a wakeful afternoon. Her change of plan this day was quite unusual.

She had left her car in the park. She returned to it and put her Marks & Spencer bags in the car boot. Then, thinking to surprise John, she set out for the Crown and Orb.

John was there indeed. Seated opposite him, at a very small table, was Pamela Bartlett. Pamela had just leant across the table to pat John's hand. What she was saying was, 'So don't worry about the silly old leylandii, John, I'll see to all that.'

Laura blinked. John hadn't seen her. She turned around and left quietly. She then drove home and put three vests and three pairs of pants into John's underwear drawer.

## 27

When David Nott came out of the hospital in which he had been treated so kindly, he went back to his flat and felt totally bereft. Every surface was covered with dust.

He had found it very easy to accept and fit into the hospital routine. It suited him. His years of soldiering had equipped him for this kind of environment. The nurses were, in his book, rather like the sergeants who had managed his life when he was a rising officer, with the same kind of bossy tenderness.

It was dreadfully lonely at home. He went out for short walks. He hadn't a dog. His children were very far away.

On a walk he passed a florist's shop which announced on its window that it subscribed to Interflora. On an impulse he sent a bunch of flowers to Laura Fenby.

He very much wanted to send the flowers but decided against identifying himself. He was not to know that Laura would imagine they might have come from John.

She was quite sure that John had not seen her at the Crown and Orb, but even so maybe he had sensed her presence? The thought did not please her. She still wondered why she had so rapidly walked away simply because John was having lunch with Pamela Bartlett. Never in her whole married life had she had reason to distrust him, so why now? She felt that she must know from whom the flowers had come.

There was only one florist's in Swanmere, a village where most gardens were thick with their own daffodils, roses and chrysanthemums in season, and year-round evergreens. David's Interflora order had been delivered by this local shop. When she learnt that the flowers had come from David, Laura was pleased on two counts. First of all that they were not from John, so at least they were not a gift to assuage his guilt, and secondly that they were from David. His was an acquaintance she had come to value, and she had feared that the way in which he had exposed his emotions had embarrassed him out of the continuance of their mild friendship.

She thought again about John, holding hands with Pamela Bartlett, across a table so small that knees must meet under it. She arranged the flowers, which looked wonderfully floristy, in a tall vase on the chest in the hall, where John must see them as he came in. He threw down his hat and coat and walked straight past, even though the vase tottered. She picked up the coat and hat and hung them away in the hall closet. John always threw his things down and left them for her to put away. She would have liked to tell him that she now qualified, in court, as having a clerk of her own.

She had no idea why David Nott had sent her the flowers. If he had wanted to coerce her into giving him further material for his newspaper articles, he would have identified himself. So it must just have been a kindness. She did not know how to handle what was on her mind.

In her long married life, the greatest insecurity Laura had ever suffered had been caused by John's perennial habit of taking at least half an hour to park the car when they went out together, so making her go unaccompanied into gatherings of people whom she was afraid she would not recognise.

In the ensuing weeks, Laura sometimes saw Pamela Bartlett in the village. Pamela always greeted her effusively, with her habitual cheek-by-cheek kisses. Laura knew herself to be behind the times in not caring for this trend. She now liked it even less when being bounced against by Pamela's breasts. Her own no longer bounced. She was torn between jealousy and wonderment at how Pamela had managed to produce two babies and still keep a couple of pink grapefruits up front. If John had a mistress, she told herself, trying to be reasonable, she could hardly expect it to be someone she liked.

John was extremely thankful to have sorted out the leylandii problem at no cost to Mr Walters, from whom he received a charming letter of thanks and a bottle of excellent port, a genuine sacrifice from a now depleted cellar.

I hate spring, thought Laura, everything green, fresh and renewed, except me. An unpleasant cold did not help her self-esteem. She dared not allow herself to feel too ill to go into court. It was there she had picked up the horrible bug anyway, from an intrepid female magistrate who considered one day in bed for childbirth acceptable, but two only allowable in the case of death.

It was at this point that Peter wrote to ask John and Laura to come to Venice for Easter. Laura felt too drab to go anywhere. In fact, she was so sorry for herself that she had no idea that she had recently hurt John's feelings by turning away from him in bed.

Although not overimbued with imagination, John Fenby was far from being entirely insensitive. He now assumed that Laura had become, now that fecundity was in the past, uninterested in making love. He was unaware that, for a woman who had had four babies in quick succession, reaching the time of life when there could definitely be no more could be an aphrodisiac in itself.

He urged Laura to agree to the little holiday in Venice. 'Get your hair done, you'll feel better,' he said helpfully. Laura was in the habit of going somewhere to have her hair cut twice a year, and otherwise washing it herself. 'I don't know where to go,' she said bleakly. She knew she was being negative, and didn't care.

'Why not ask Pamela Bartlett where she goes? Her hair always looks nice,' said John. Then he wondered why Laura went up to London for the day and came back having spent fifty pounds on a hairdo that didn't suit her, and carrying a Harrods bag containing a dress that didn't suit her either.

Peter was happy in his life with the Pizzero family at the Hotel Iris. The past was behind him. He loved them all, particularly Fabiola, clever, pretty Fabiola, whom he helped with her studies. He thought of her as a child. Passion, he believed, was something he had long left behind him. He regarded himself as a safe and ancient companion for dear Maria's little daughter.

It being Easter and the city full of tourists, he was glad to be able to book his parents into the Hotel Iris. Giovanni made no foolish protests about accepting them as paying customers. This did not prevent him from being wildly generous with the grappa, a bottle of which *digestif* passed freely round the dinner table every night.

A couple of little ones would nod off on any available lap, and Fabiola always sat beside Peter.

'I hope Peter isn't going to fall in love with that nice little girl,' said John. 'She's far too young.'

'It wouldn't be the first time,' said Laura, emboldened by two glasses of grappa, 'that older men have fallen in love with younger women.'

'I suppose you're right,' said John, and vouchsafed no more.

Laura felt friendly towards these happy people. She would have liked to ask Maria if *her* husband had a mistress. But Maria's very few words of English, and Laura's even fewer words of Italian, precluded conversation of greater moment than the menu, babies, and where to shop. In any case, she would never have been impertinent enough to ask such a question.

Maria was somewhat overawed, at first, by Laura. That Peter's papa was an attorney was easy to understand. But that his mother should be a *magistrato* (for Maria, there was no such word as *magistrata*) was daunting. However, Laura bore no resemblance to the ladies she had seen on old reruns of *Rumpole of the Bailey*, in their wigs and gowns. She was a mother, like herself.

'Peter,' said Maria, 'is good. Good and kind. Kind to my children.'

'And you have all been so kind to him. He has had some sadness, and you have helped him so much, to get over it all.'

Small glib phrases were all that could be said of a failed marriage and a disastrous love affair, not to mention her own conviction that Peter, as her first-born, had suffered from her pathetic inexperience as a mother. Laura was almost as much in awe of Maria as Maria had been of her. To her, Maria was a woman who had been born with an in-built ability to be a wife and mother.

'You have grandchildren,' said Maria. 'I also, one day, I hope.'

By the time the Fenbys went home, the humanities had melted all traces of awe between the two women. Laura kissed Maria goodbye with genuine affection. She was also kissed and hugged by Fabiola, who stood with Peter under the vine outside the little hotel, waving to his parents as they left.

# 28

Laura found that, contrary to her expectations, her visit to Venice had done her good.

Although conversation with Maria was necessarily limited, she believed that this overtly placid woman was a tougher fighter than appeared, on the surface, to be the case. She obviously loved Giovanni. Equally obviously, she had, in her apparently acquiescent way, the upper hand.

The upper hand was not something Laura had ever sought. She had seen no need for it. To her, marriage had always been marriage, not a battlefield.

Her relationship with her mother was rather like an ongoing, unwinnable war, of course, and it was way beyond Laura's nature to be even half as unpleasant to Veronica as Veronica had always been to her. However, with other things to worry about, she found herself taking less and less notice of Veronica's acid tongue. This had no modifying effect on the old woman, who remained as complacently destructive as ever. When Laura, only half listening, smiled and murmured quietly, 'Oh really,' and, 'I dare say,' she simply put it down to her daughter's dullness, and gave poor old Miss Fawcett-Smythe what for later.

Although Laura felt certain that John was having an

affair with Pamela Bartlett, it was not in her nature to play tricks. But straightforward as she was, she still found it impossible to ask her husband if he was up to something.

Her resumed friendship with David Nott became a comfort and a fillip to her self-esteem. She had written to thank him for the flowers, and they had met for a lunchtime coffee. He was still looking pale from his illness, and she exclaimed about it. He described what had happened, and she sympathised with him.

'It should have been I who sent you the flowers,' she said. 'You must have been feeling very low.'

'I think that's why I sent them,' he said meekly.

'You should have let me know. That's what friends are for,' she said evenly. 'And that's what we are, aren't we?' she added briskly.

Although David, in his loneliness, could easily have fallen in love with her, the fact that the one thing she never mentioned to him was her suspicion that her husband had a mistress prevented such a fantasy from developing.

Now and then they would have tea together. It made an agreeable five o'clock for both of them. 'It's nice,' said David, putting butter and jam on a scone as they sat on wobbly chairs in one of those copper-panned Ye Olde Tea Shoppes that still so anomalously survive in English country towns, 'not to drink.'

'Are you afraid of drinking too much?' asked Laura.

'Certainly. You've seen me doing it. You came to my rescue on that occasion.'

'But I wouldn't say you had a problem.' Laura had seen drink and drug problems enough in the court, but David Nott bore no resemblance, in her view, to any of those hopeless and helpless people. She saw him as a capable man, good at his job, and taking great care of his ailing wife.

It was now the beautiful time of year. The bluebells still carpeted the woods, beneath the chestnuts and the birches. The beech trees were at that stage when their leaves still delicately permit the sun to shine through them, so that they look like the shimmering silver-green silk velvet of long-ago children's party dresses. It was agreeable to take an early evening walk.

At this time neither Laura nor David was anxious to get home. Home for him was the empty flat, and the whisky bottle he determined to keep at arm's length for as long as he possibly could. Home for Laura was now a place in which she found it difficult to behave naturally. She tried to introduce the name of Pamela Bartlett into a conversation, but was unable to do so. John, for his part, never mentioned her. The business of the leylandii was over and done, and he saw no need to discuss, at home, a slightly mean act by one neighbour against another that he had managed to put right. So, with the name unspoken, Laura was left simply to wonder and fester.

David found Laura's company increasingly enjoyable and easy. The little urge he had felt towards her gave way to a comfortable exchange of confidences. Laura asked him the names of his children.

'Mark and Sara. Sara is the older of the two. Fiona had a rough time when she was born, and it would have been hell for her to go through it again, but she would have if I'd asked her. She was like that, she simply had to do everything she thought it was right to do.'

'And she did all the upbringing of the children?' asked Laura, and added, 'Well, actually so did I.'

'Was John not a helpful father?'

'Well, he was no nappy-changer. He'd take the boys out into the garden to start to learn to play cricket. Peter irritated him because he couldn't catch a ball; he was hopelessly unathletic. And Luke irritated him because he was far too good. Everything was always easy for Luke. Luckily, my girls were pretty, so that was all right.'

'I haven't an idea where either Sara or Mark are now. Oh, I know they're in Australia and India, but I don't know exactly where. You've done better.'

'I don't know. Peter's had a divorce and a disastrous love affair. Judy's all right. She had the toughest start, but now she's happily married and has a dear baby. Luke's a bit itinerant. He's got a girlfriend, older than him. I like her, but I sometimes worry that the relationship doesn't look to have much of a future, although they seem very happy together. And Ann and her husband seem to be going through a bad patch.' And so am I, she did not say. She could not talk of her doubts, her fear of Pamela's pretty body and its attractions for any man, never mind a man whose wife was feeling old and unattractive, so she turned the subject.

'Wouldn't you think it a good idea, in the circumstances, to try and find Mark and Sara? It might be a great help to Fiona.'

'You're right. I must do something about it. I'd like to see them myself, anyway. It's time I made up to them for the past. But tell me about your Ann and her husband. What's the problem?'

'They've got a restaurant. Ann became a chef, and that's how they met in the first place. My mother was horrified at Ann becoming a kitchen maid, as she put it, and marrying a scullion. My mother really can be awful at times. But I don't let it worry me now. I used to get dreadfully upset when she lived with us, but it's much easier, now that I just visit her at Cathay Manor.'

'So I take it that she regarded it as a déclassé marriage?'

'She did, indeed. And I daren't let her know what's happened now. It's one of those unlucky things. Poor Ann wasn't well. She had a miscarriage, and as far as I can make out, Len had a brief affair with one of the waitresses while she was still feeling ill. I suppose one has to understand a man's needs, doesn't one?'

John Fenby was bewildered to find his wife so distant. The house was in order, and meals were punctual. He kissed her when he came home, and she allowed it. He asked her how things were going in the court, and she said, 'Fine.' He realised that becoming a magistrate had taken Laura into a new sphere, but he found it hard to bear that he no longer seemed to come first with her. Even when the children were at their most time-consuming age, and the house at times a shambles, he had never felt neglected. She had certainly been snappy with him when his mother-in-law had been living in the house. She was not snappy now, just frighteningly polite. He simply could not imagine what must be wrong. Had she been a woman like that Pamela Bartlett, one would wonder if there was someone else. She was still quite attractive enough, God knew.

The work he had always enjoyed, the position he had occupied with unquestioning content for so many years, suddenly began to seem dull and unworthwhile. Maybe he had become a dull dog himself. He was grey, and his trousers had all got too tight. At one time he had been censorious about Peter's behaviour. Now he envied his elder son for getting out of the rut while there was still time.

## 29

Peter Fenby was happy. He had the money he earned from his teaching, and he now also had had a small allowance pressed upon him by Larry and Judy Cunningham. Larry had insisted upon this, and had written to him to explain that it was in his, Larry's, interest that Peter should maintain a foothold in Venice.

'I am hoping,' he wrote, 'that you will advise me when I want to buy goods for our store. And Judy and I will always want to bring Laura Ann over. She now calls herself Lann.'

Giovanni and Maria were delighted that Fabiola was learning to speak such good English. It was their fondest hope that she would go to college, and maybe even become a teacher. All Italian waiters spoke scrappy English with an American accent, but their girl spoke proper English. Fabiola was allowed to go anywhere she wished, under the paternal protection of their friend Peter.

Peter, they knew, would never let her come to any harm. Chaperoned by Peter, Fabiola was safe from the approaches of the wretched boys, Italian and foreigners alike, who would seek to have their wicked way with so pretty a young girl. They were right, inasmuch as that no boy got a look-in with Fabiola. Fabiola was in love with Peter.

On a hot day, walking across St Mark's Square, Fabiola was jostled by two very large blonde girls carrying back-packs. One of the packs hit her hard on her face, and she was almost felled to the ground. Peter grabbed her with both arms. The blow to her face had hurt, and there were tears pouring down her cheeks. He gave her a comforting kiss. Her response was not what he had expected. He had not been aware of Fabiola as a passionate creature. Nor had he known that there was still passion in him. He was shocked into immediate stillness.

'Come and let me get you some coffee,' he said. Fabiola looked up at him. Her cheek was already puffy, and one eye was closing. He decided to take her home.

'Have you anything for bruises?' he asked Maria. 'Some clumsy great tourists banged into our poor little one with their back-packs. They don't look where they are going. She got a horrid bump on her face.'

Maria got arnica, and took Fabiola on to her lap as though she was still one of the babies. The little ones came up and patted her. 'Poor Fabby.' With all the petting and cuddling that was going on, Maria failed to notice how Fabiola reached out her hand and clung to Peter's.

Very soon the bruise began to colour. Maria put Fabiola to bed, where she lay and cried, partly with the pain but mostly because of what she knew she looked like. Having work to do, Maria asked Peter to go and sit with her. 'She's crying because she thinks she looks ugly. But with you, she won't mind. She is at ease with you as she is with her own papa. She is so fond of you. We all are. If you had been here when she was born, you would have been her godfather.'

Peter refrained from asking what their priest would have said about giving a Catholic baby a Protestant godfather. He merely went up to Fabiola's bedroom, took a chair, seated himself as far from the bed as he could get, and reminded himself that, in Maria's view, he was old enough to be Fabiola's father.

As the summer heated up, Fabiola's bruises gradually faded, and the family talked more and more about their hopes and pleasure in the prospect of Fabiola's college education. Franco, next in age, was as delighted as anyone, since Fabiola had taken the pressure off him. Franco was a dear boy, with no academic aims in the world. Sometimes he thought of being a croupier, sometimes a sports commentator on the TV, sometimes of going to London as a waiter, and getting very rich on the enormous tips he imagined all customers in that distant city would hand out. He believed he spoke English. 'No problem!' 'Have a nice day!' and 'Yes, I speak English,' was the extent of his vocabulary.

Peter tried very hard to keep out of Fabiola's way. Fabiola, alone in her bedroom, cried herself to sleep with love for him. For his part, Peter ached to make love to her. He had not known the sensation of loving for such a long time. Sex, in his recent life, had been an occasional pastime, a gratification that did no harm to anybody; a sort of genital handshake.

His longing for Fabiola was a melding of body and mind. She was fairer than her parents, honey-coloured in comparison to them. When she took her baby

171

brother on her lap, she had a way of bending her head down to kiss him that made her look like one of the better frescos of the Madonna.

Never before in his life had Peter felt the sort of love that wants to create a child.

Never before had Fabiola, accustomed to the popularity and following the nature of her prettiness had always engendered, been in love. Boys are silly, she had always thought. But now, this was a man in her life. She had come only slowly into this state of realisation. She had, at first, scarcely noticed the tall, distinguished, grown-up Englishman who had drifted into her family world.

Throughout the summer Fabiola was such a useful help in the Hotel Iris that her father said to her, with pretended ruefulness, that he didn't know how they were going to manage without her when she went away to college.

'I am not going,' said Fabiola.

Maria, hearing this remark, announced, 'Of course you are going. Such nonsense – you are not going to sacrifice all your chances for us. Franco can work here perfectly well. He's a lazy boy and he can't cook, but he can do plenty. I shall make him do plenty. And we have Peter. Peter is the greatest help to us. You don't have to stay here. You must not.'

'I don't want to go to college,' said Fabiola firmly.

Maria, who always spoke fast, spoke as slowly as she could. 'Not go to college? Not become a teacher, when you have learnt already so much from Peter, an educated man? Not go to college, when we are prepared to make sacrifices for you to go? Why not?'

'I have other plans,' said Fabiola.

172

## 30

It had been a very hot day, and particularly hot in court. It was extraordinary that so high-ceilinged a chamber could be so airless. The cases had gone on all morning and most of the afternoon. For some obscure reason, the roof of the court in which Laura was sitting was a favourite landing place for seagulls, no matter how far they had to fly to get there. The perpetual noise they made added to the sense-dulling effect of stuffiness and a succession of long-drawn-out motoring offences.

On this occasion Laura was, for the first time, chairman of the bench. She found it quite awesome to see each dusty solicitor enter and bow to what it was she represented. Rather shyly, she inclined her own head in return.

There were only two drug cases on this August day. One was that of a forty-eight-year-old woman, whose hard-faced aspect might once have been the face of a pretty young girl. But that would have been very long ago. The other was a young man of nineteen, only just old enough to be in adult court. The police had caught him peddling to school children.

Had his working life not been so sinister, he would have been merely a pathetic character. 'Madam,' said his defending solicitor, 'Mr Smith was himself addicted to cocaine while still a child. His habit results in his need of a great deal of money.' Mr Smith could scarcely read or write. He had been brought up (if you could call it that) by a mother who lived alone between brief liaisons which had resulted in the arrival of further half-related children.

Laura glanced down at the press seats. David Nott was there, almost nodding off over his notebook.

'Mr Smith,' continued the defending solicitor, 'is living with a girlfriend who has a child. His girlfriend is a prostitute, and Mr Smith has a child of his own, by another, previous partner. Madam, he is striving to support this child.'

After court, Laura found herself walking to the car park side by side with David. 'You look whacked,' he said. 'What about some tea?'

'I'd love to, but I'd better not. I ought to go and see my mother before I go home.'

'And then you'll be getting the dinner. I hope John realises what a lucky man he is.'

'How is Fiona?' asked Laura.

'Not too bad. She sometimes asks me why she can't come home, but I think she forgets about it as soon as I've gone.'

'Have you had any joy trying to find Mark and Sara?'

'Beginnings of . . . I got hold of an old friend of Sara's, through her school. You must be horrified that I know so little about my own children.'

'I don't know,' said Laura, 'sometimes I think I know a bit too much about mine.' This remark was to turn out to be true before the evening was out.

The visit to Veronica was not too bad. She had that morning reduced Miss Fawcett-Smythe to tears, with which easy feat Laura was regaled. 'Such a silly creature. All in a twitter about this new man who's come here. "You're not a girl, and you haven't been for sixty years," I told her for her own good. And what do you think she said?' There was no need to ask, Laura was going to hear what poor foolish Miss Fawcett-Smythe had said, whether she wished or not. ' "I was considered quite pretty at one time." ' The remainder of Veronica's put-down of Miss Fawcett-Smythe filled visiting time.

Laura got home, longing for a cool bath before starting the dinner. Getting the dinner, eating it, watching television until after the news, and then going up to bed still went on every night, to the accompaniment of nervously well-mannered conversation. Laura wished John would make love to her. John longed at least to cuddle her, and neither of them knew how to go about it.

Before she could get upstairs, the telephone rang. Laura answered it, wondering if John was going to be late home. But it was not John. It was Ann.

'Mummy?' said Ann. Ever since Len had begun to do so, Ann had always called Laura 'Mum'. This reversion to childhood 'Mummy' was an alarm bell ringing in Laura's sensitive ear.

'Darling? Are you all right? Is J. L. all right?'

'J. L. is fine. It's Len. I don't know what to do.' Out it all came. Len's brief infidelity had been a stone thrown into a pond only to make ever-widening rings. He had sworn to Ann that it was over, and had never meant anything anyway. 'But that can't be true,

Mummy. I've made him get rid of her from the restaurant, but he goes to see her, I'm certain of it.'

'Are you sure? And if he does, when it comes down to it, is it more important than everything you have together? He loves you, I know he does.'

'I think I ought to divorce him.'

'Just for one infidelity? He wouldn't be the first husband to do something silly. Do think about it more, darling. Talk to him, please.' What good advice I'm giving, thought Laura, ironically.

'I have. He says it's finished and he isn't seeing her. But I don't believe him.'

'Ann, this isn't like you. You've always been my sensible girl. It used to be Judy I worried over, but I've always been so happy about you and Len. So has Daddy.' Laura could feel sweat trickling down her sides and the backs of her legs. If only she could peel off her tights. Under the black serge skirt she had been wearing since eight o'clock this morning, her legs felt as though they were encased in burning barbed wire. 'I can't bear,' she continued, 'to think of you throwing away everything you and Len have put together over the years. And what about J. L.?'

'I'm certainly not going to let Len have him, not if he's going to be with bloody Bella. I wouldn't let my child anywhere near her.'

'But I don't believe he wants bloody Bella,' said Laura. She was troubled to know what to say next. She feared that poor Ann's wretched miscarriage and subsequent depression had a lot to do with this, and blamed herself for not having been more observant at the time. In the end, knowing that there was no question of her taking on J. L. herself, she said, 'How will you manage?'

'I'll bring him up by myself. Hundreds of women do. I'm a chef, for heaven's sake. Chefs, especially good ones like me, can always get work.'

If only, thought Laura, she was here, instead of on the telephone, I'd give her a good smack and then a kiss. At this point, she heard John's key in the lock of the front door. 'I'm terribly sorry,' she said, 'I do want to talk to you much more. But Daddy's just come in, so I'll have to go for the moment. Shall I ring you later?'

'No, don't. It's all right.' Ann rang off, bitterly envying her mother, so safe and so secure with Daddy. All right for her, all passion spent and a pillar of society and married life.

This not being overcoat weather, John came in, took off his jacket and threw it at the banister-knob, which it missed and fell to the floor. Laura slowly returned the receiver to its cradle.

'Who were you talking to?' asked John.

'Ann.'

'She's all right, I hope. Nothing wrong?'

'She's fine.'

'I'm sorry I'm a bit late. Something went on longer than I expected.'

'It doesn't matter. I've had a long day myself. And then I had a chat with David Nott, that journalist, you know. And then I had to go and see my mother.'

'Is Veronica all right?'

'She's pretty well. Very happy, really.'

'I'm going to get myself a drink,' said John. 'Can I get you anything?'

'I'll have a bath first,' said Laura.

'What's for dinner?' asked John.

After dinner John went into the sitting room, switched on the TV, and sat down to watch. Usually, these days, Laura would join him and allow whatever boring programme was on to substitute for the communication which now did not take place between them. Soaps and the world's disasters transcended family affairs.

Tonight she said, 'John, do you mind if I switch off? I want to talk to you.'

'All right.' John biffed the remote control and the screen went dark.

'I told you Ann rang. I have to tell you about it. She's talking of getting a divorce.'

'What on earth for?'

Knowing that John was about to huff and puff about young people these days, Laura cut in, 'Well, you know how odd she and Len were over Christmas? It seems that Len got too friendly with a waitress, well, actually had an affair with her.'

'Doesn't this happen an awful lot in this day and age? But I suppose Ann's old-fashioned.'

This might have been the moment to bring the conversation round to her own suspicions, but somehow Laura just couldn't do it. The nearest she could get was to say, 'She's like me in some ways. Len was the first man in her life, as you were in mine. She's terribly hurt. I don't blame her. But I do hope and pray she'll forgive him. They belong together. And, apart from that, there's J. L. He'd be a single-parent child.'

'That's not uncommon, God knows,' said John.

'More's the pity. I had a case in court today, a lad peddling drugs.' She told John about the case of Mr

178

Smith. He listened with an attentiveness he had not often shown, asking questions and paying attention to her answers. Later on, he made them both a nightcap, and they went up to bed. They kissed each other good night, and lay side by side, touching.

John, thinking Laura was asleep, whispered, 'Do you know how much I love you? You are the centre of my world.'

Laura said nothing but stroked his face.

Next day, Laura went into the village to do some shopping. In the High Street Pamela Bartlett swept up to her, reaching out to plant her usual kisses. Laura stepped back, smiled politely and said, 'Good morning, Pamela. How are you?' To herself she said, I don't give a damn if my husband *is* up to something with you. He loves me, so there.

In a decisive mood, she made up her mind that she would go and see Ann and Len, and give the pair of them a piece of her mind. They must learn that they were grown-ups with a child, and they'd jolly well better sort themselves out.

# 31

It was not in Luke Fenby's nature to get depressed. As a baby, the youngest of the family, his naturally jolly disposition had flourished. He had been breast-fed until he was one year old, a menu he had ordered for himself. Laura, struggling to try and create some sort of household order, and with her two little girls coming in from school every afternoon for tea, simply stuffed him up her jumper as she went about her tasks, and rather enjoyed the proximity of his friendly little body.

Although Mary Trent had no intention of marrying Luke – she declared herself to be too selfish to marry a poor man – she was well aware that she enjoyed his company more than that of any other man of her acquaintance. Luke's ways didn't bother her in the least. Sometimes he worked, sometimes he didn't. He could always get jobs. Luke could talk his way into anything. At one time Mary was tempted to get him into the advertising agency where she starred, but sense prevailed, and she didn't do it.

What she did do was to allow him the free run of her flat, a lazy decision that gave her a lot of fun. Her cleaner, a snarly crone in the ordinary way, adored Luke enough to iron his shirts and quite often hers as well, since hers were so well cut she thought they were his. Luke, though disorderly, was not lazy, nor was he too proud to sing for his supper and, frequently, to cook it.

It was a hot evening, just into August. Mary's flat had a little balcony, facing west over a communal garden. The evening sun illuminated a bottle of cold white wine and some grilled chicken thighs. 'I'll tell you something,' said Luke, 'my sister Ann has been thinking of splitting with Len. Ma told me.'

'She must be very upset,' said Mary.

'She is. But she's still very hopeful that they'll get it together again. She adores J. L. so much so that the one thing she is determined upon is that he isn't going to be a single-parent child. She told me about cases she's dealt with in court, and she can't bear the thought of Ann and Len divorcing.'

'You see, I told you. Getting married isn't a good idea in the first place,' said Mary, picking up a piece of chicken. She took a small bite, and suddenly spat it out into her hand.

'Good Lord, it isn't that bad, is it?' said Luke.

'I've got a ghastly pain. I'm going to be sick.' Mary left the balcony. Luke, following her, found the bathroom door closed. He knew Mary too well to burst in on her. When she emerged, white-faced, he stood back while she went to the bedroom and lay down.

'Would you like to be left alone?' he asked.

'No, I wouldn't. I'm in agony. I don't know what it is. I'm never ill. I've never been ill. I don't understand.'

'Shall I get your doctor?'

'I haven't got a doctor. I hate doctors. I only ever go near them to get a prescription for the pill.'

'Oh damn, I wish my Mum was here,' wailed Luke.

'Well, she isn't. And I'm dying.' Like most people who customarily enjoy rude health Mary, faced with appendicitis, which was what her ailment turned out to be, was convinced by the time Luke got her into the hospital that she was walking down death's corridor.

Luke, visiting, was told by the staff nurse that the operation had been simple and successful and that Mrs Trent was 'coming along beautifully, Mr Trent.' Luke forbore to admit that he was not Mr Trent.

Mary did not consider herself to be coming along beautifully. 'Look what they've done to my belly,' she wailed. 'Look at this fucking tinware.' The tinware was a row of clips. 'I'll never get this flat again. Who's going to fancy me with a façade like a sow's tits?'

Her room, which was private, was filled with flowers. They came from everyone in her advertising agency, and there was even a bunch from her ex-husband. Luke decided not to compete. He, Luke, was the one who loved her. To that end, he tidied up the flat in her absence, put all the towels and sheets into the washing machine, and made up the bed to be comfortable for her when she should return.

Once she had closed death's door behind her, Mary was bored stiff. She was scarcely out of hospital two days before she went back to work. There her managing director, who was fond of her, and had borne with fortitude her refusal to go to bed with him, decreed that some leave was necessary. 'I don't feel holiday-fied,' she said crossly to Luke. 'And I'm certainly not going anywhere near a beach with this mess,' indicating her stomach.

'You needn't. I'd like to go to Venice; I haven't seen

my big brother for ages. Come with me. We can stay at his place. It won't cost much.'

'Yes, Venice would be lovely. But what's this place of your brother's like? I'm not a back-packer when I'm well, and I've just been very ill.'

'It'll be all right. Pete knows the people well. Come on, do let's go. If you will, I tell you what I'll do. I'll get a job when we come back, and I'll stick to it. So now?'

'I'll believe that when I see it. No, keep your hands to yourself, it hurts too much.'

It was early September when Luke and Mary came out of the railway station, and found themselves, instantly and gloriously, in Venice. Peter was there to meet them as they got off the vaporetto, and he and Luke carried the luggage to the Hotel Iris. Most of it was Mary's. 'We've given you a nice room,' said Peter.

'*A* room?' said Mary. 'Will they mind? They're Catholics, surely?'

'Yes,' said Peter, 'but they're not completely archaic.' In fact Maria and Giovanni simply did not ask any guests about their private status. They were all foreigners, anyway, and had nothing to do with Maria and Giovanni's views of family.

Hands were shaken all round. 'What a pretty child,' said Mary, meeting Fabiola.

Fabiola took an instant liking to the English lady. Being in love with Peter, she was extremely glad that Mary was Luke's property, as she saw it. Quite soon, she was taking her new friend shopping and feeling, happily, as though they were already sisters-in-law.

'Is Peter sleeping with that little girl?' Mary asked

Luke. 'I hope, for his own sake, not. The parents would kill him, believe you me.'

'Let's hope he isn't then,' said Luke, 'My poor brother's had enough troubles without having a contract put out on him.'

Mary spoke no Italian, so Fabiola's considerable command of English was very useful to her. That Fabiola, as they went about, always closely linked arms with her made her a little uncomfortable at first. Mary was not keen on physical contact with her own sex. However she decided philosophically that the customs in Italy were different. 'You speak very good English,' she said.

'I learn it from Peter. I learn everything from Peter. He is wonderful, isn't he?'

Seeing which way this was pointing Mary, knowing the girl was scarcely nineteen, asked, 'What are you going to do with your life? But you must still be studying.'

'My parents are cross with me about that. They wanted me to go to college, but I don't want to go. I'm going to marry Peter.'

'You are far too young to get married.'

'No, my mother was hardly any older than I am when she got married.'

In the face of this determination, Mary felt herself stumped. She wondered whether to tell Fabiola about her own early marriage and subsequent divorce. She also wondered whether to tell her at how young an age Peter's sister Ann had begun her life with Len, and how that marriage was now in trouble.

She also wondered whether to warn her that marrying a divorced Protestant would be, in this family, a sin so dreadful as to be out of the question. In the end, she said nothing and bought Fabiola a turquoise necklace.

'Pete,' said Luke to his brother, 'do you realise that that little girl is in love with you? She wants to marry you. She told Mary, and Mary told me. What are you going to do about it?'

'Oh God,' said Peter. 'I don't know what to do. I do love her. There's something so sweet about her.'

'Could you get your divorce turned into an annulment, and then convert to Catholicism?' It was Luke's talent for pragmatism that made him a happy man. That and the optimism with which he convinced himself that what Luke wanted, Luke would get, although he never worried for too long if he didn't.

## 32

'id you manage to talk some sense into them?' asked John, when Laura got back from her visit to Ann and Len. They were sitting out in the garden, drinking a spritzer. Much to Laura's surprise John had announced that a cold supper was at her disposal, prepared by him. For the first time in his life John had gone to the supermarket, where he had bought a tub of coronation chicken, some French bread, and sundry salads of olives and feta, coleslaw, and a very venturesome one of beans and what looked like seaweed. By the time they had abandoned the soda water, done justice to the white wine on its own, and reached a runny Brie, Laura decided that John's catering was substantially better than her own.

'I don't know. Ann's terribly touchy at the moment. I asked her to try and look at it as though it were two other people, but all she would say was that it wasn't two other people, it was her and Len, and Len would never have done that if he loved her. I wish to God she'd never found out about it.'

'*Is* it still going on? With the girl, I mean.'

'I'm sure it's not. I talked to Len. He's absolutely miserable, doesn't want to lose her, and all Ann will say is that's only because she's useful in the restaurant.

And he keeps saying he doesn't know how to tell her that that isn't so at all.'

'Would you like me to see if I can do anything?' asked John.

'Hmm. Would you be tactful?'

'Of course I'd be tactful. I'd knock their heads together.'

'Perhaps you're right. I didn't seem to do much good.' Then, maybe it was the wine – John had opened a bottle of red to go with the Brie – that made Laura continue, and say at last, 'John, have you been having an affair with Pamela Bartlett?'

'What makes you ask that?'

'I saw you with her at the Crown and Orb.'

'You saw me having lunch, and you didn't come over?'

'You were holding hands.'

'To be more precise, she was holding my hands. It was not of my seeking. I had no intention of taking her out to lunch. She had an appointment with me in the morning, and she arrived late, so as it got to one o'clock, I hadn't much option.'

'What was she seeing you about? Getting a divorce?' The sun had set, the moon had risen. It was a glorious evening.

'Don't be silly, darling, you know perfectly well I don't do divorce. I had asked her to come and see me, because I wanted her to persuade Kenneth to cut back the leylandii he'd planted, and I didn't want it to cost the poor old boy next door anything. He has very little money. And I was pretty sure I could get her to do what I wanted. You know she had this idea she wanted to be a magistrate, and that I might be useful to her.'

'You wily old thing. But you did fancy her a bit, didn't you?'

'She's very attractive, I grant you. I defy any man not to stare down that cleavage. But no. Apart from the fact that if I were going to have an affair I'd have more sense than to have it on my own doorstep, I have no intention of doing any such thing. It would be wrong.'

By now it was deep night, although the moon was still riding up the sky. 'You must have wanted somebody other than me sometimes,' Laura insisted.

'No, I have not,' was all John would say. It was not in him to put into words his belief that forsaking all others was a tenet of marriage that must be obeyed, and that he, especially when the babies were little and demanding, had fought the temptation to stray that is almost inevitable in a normal man when his wife's body is not only given over to her children, but its appearance disimproved by that service. Sometimes that had been hard, but now he could say with conviction, 'You can't seriously think I'd fancy a silly woman like Pamela when I have you, can you?'

'I did think so. Let's face it, when a woman sees her husband holding hands over a table, and those tables at the Crown and Orb are built for touching knees as well, she's apt to get a bit iffy about it, wouldn't you think? And I did.'

'Why didn't you say something sooner?'

'First of all, I couldn't. And then later, it didn't seem to matter. Not as much as having you does.'

'I'm glad to hear you say so,' said John, trying to sound lighter than he felt. 'I did wonder, a bit, about your friend David Nott.'

Where once Laura would have been fussing about, carrying in plates and bottles, she now remained riveted to her seat. She completely forgot that this conversation had started out with the problems of Ann and Len. She had always loved and respected her husband but, maybe because the few years more of his age had seemed awe-inspiring when she was a young bride, she had never, until now, felt herself to be his equal. 'David Nott? Yes, I like him very much. It's a friendship I truly value. We talk to each other, and I think I've been able to help him a little. His wife is in a nursing home, and he has lost touch with his children. He is lonely, you see, where you are not. So I hope you will–' she was going to say 'allow' but changed her mind, and said instead – 'understand that I have a friendship I have made for myself.'

'It's really changed your life, being a beak, hasn't it?' said John.

'I hope you don't think it's changed me too much,' said Laura.

'It's changed you, yes. Have you looked at yourself, when you are suited up and going to court?'

'Only to see if I'm neat and tidy.'

'Well, let me tell you that subfusc is very sexy on you.'

'Well I never! What next?'

'Bed,' said John.

In the morning, Laura found the garden in chaos. Something, presumably a fox, had done the clearing up. The lawn was covered with broken glass and crockery, and the garden table tipped over on its side. And neither of them had heard a thing.

★

John Fenby left his wife asleep having a much-deserved lie-in, and got out the car. He found himself driving too fast, and slowed down. This was no time to get himself killed.

When he arrived at the restaurant, he found Ann waiting on tables. 'Can't someone else do that?' he said.

'Daddy! What are you doing here?'

'I've come to see you. Stop that and sit down.'

'I can't,' said Ann crossly. 'We don't have a waitress any more.'

'Then I'll wait until you finish.'

At half-past two John Fenby, adopting the dispassionate and masterful manner usually reserved for court appearances, ordered his daughter and son-in-law to seat themselves at a table in the empty restaurant. What he did then, he described later to Laura as 'having it out with them'.

Len was told with some firmness that he was a fool. 'Heavens, boy, anyone can understand what you wanted. It was only sex. I haven't forgotten my own youth, you know.' Ann looked shocked. 'And, Ann, you should have explained to Len what was wrong with you.'

'He knew perfectly well,' said Ann sulkily. 'I was depressed. I'd lost my baby. And all he wanted to do was to get me into bed again.' She had at last begun to forget that it was to her own father that she was speaking. 'And it hurt like hell.'

Len put in his word. 'Why didn't you say, instead of just pushing me away? That wasn't fair. I'm sorry about what I did, please believe me. Actually, you ought to feel sorry for Bella. She doesn't mean a thing to me, I've kept trying to tell you.'

'You probably don't know this, Ann,' said John, 'but I've just found out that your mother, quite recently, thought *I* was having an affair.'

'*You*, Daddy?' Ann was really shocked.

'You're quite right. But it's what Mummy thought, and even so she was prepared to forgive me. So come on, grow up.'

# 33

Four months later, early in the evening, Miss Fawcett-Smythe took her secateurs and went out into the garden to get holly and greenery for the Christmas decorations. It was her favourite time of year. She never left Cathay Manor; she had nowhere else to go. Every year the fees went up. But Miss Fawcett-Smythe was grateful that she could still afford to pay them, out of the income derived from the sale of her parental home.

The mother to whom she owed her perpetual state of spinsterhood had prepared her well for the role of lady-in-waiting to Veronica Chadwick, 'my dear friend'. And her anciently virginal girlishness had equally prepared her for the enjoyment of the company of Clive Beresford, the new arrival, who had once been an actor and who had written a play which had never been performed. Mr Beresford spoke of youthful conquests of the fair sex, but had never married. He could play the grand piano in the drawing room, and sing 'A bachelor gay am I,' while Miss Fawcett-Smythe stood by and admired.

Miss Fawcett-Smythe was delighted that dear Veronica had decided, this year, to spend Christmas Day at Cathay: 'My daughter wants me to go to her, but it was so uncomfortable and noisy last time that I really prefer not to go.' And Mr Beresford would also be there on Christmas Day. 'I look forward to pulling a cracker with you, dear Florence,' he had said. Florence was looking forward to Christmas Day as never before. The great fire would be burning in the flagged hall, and her decorations would be the *pièce de résistance*.

Unfortunately, or perhaps fortunately, Miss Fawcett-Smythe spent Christmas Day on her deathbed. An early onset of snow and frost had given way to mud. While reaching for a particularly desirable sprig of holly, she had slipped and fallen. She had managed to struggle back indoors, deliriously thinking that after a little rest she would go out and bring in the boughs she had cut. So silent was she about the pain of what was actually a broken hip that no one noticed anything wrong until it was too late, and she was approaching her maker by way of the old person's friend, pneumonia. Thanks to the Lord and his infinite mercy, Miss Fawcett-Smythe was spared the knowledge that her income would only have lasted another two months. And, thanks to her own fortitude, she was also spared dying in hospital, being found dead in her bed by the maid. The coffin was smuggled out of the back door so as not to upset the extant residents.

'Poor old thing,' said Veronica to Clive, 'she should never have attempted to go out. But she always was silly.'

'She was not. She was a very sweet girl, the sort I wished I had married.'

The rebuke sharpened Veronica up no end, and she

decided that from henceforward she would take on Clive Beresford as knight–consort.

'What,' John had asked Laura, 'do you want to do about Christmas? Would you like to go away?'

'I don't think so. I'm very fond of my home. Perhaps it would be a good thing if we asked Ann and Len to come.'

'No. Leave them alone.'

On Christmas Eve, the Bartletts gave a large party. Along with anybody who was anybody in Swanmere, the Fenbys were invited. After the thaw that had been the death of Miss Fawcett-Smythe, it suddenly became cold and frosty. Walking home after the party through the crisp fresh air, Laura began to laugh.

'What's so funny?' asked John.

'You can't have heard what I heard. Pamela!'

'What about her?'

'Surely you saw him? The fat man. His name's Hirshman, he hasn't been here long. He's a publisher. So dear Pamela's gone off the magistracy, thank goodness. What she's going to do now is write a book when she gets the time, and when Mr Hirshman has told her what to write about and how to do it, or perhaps more likely to do it for her, by the way she was wiggling at him. Bad luck, darling.'

For the first time since their eldest's birth, John and Laura spent Christmas Day entirely on their own. Laura invited David Nott to join them, but he was obliged to refuse, as he would be travelling at that time.

'Where are you going?' asked Laura.

'To Australia. I found out at last where Sara is. She's married and she lives in Melbourne. I've spoken to her on the telephone, so she knows, now, about her mother. She has a boy of seven, and she's expecting another baby.'

'So you *are* a grandfather. Has Fiona taken it in?'

'I haven't said anything to her about it,' said David sadly. 'There's no point. I discussed it with Matron. Sara can't possibly travel, the new baby is due very soon and she lost one earlier.'

It was, in fact, Matron who had persuaded him to go. 'I promise you, Mr Nott, Mrs Nott will be perfectly happy with us.' In fact David was already aware that Fiona, when she was distressed, was more inclined to call for firm, kind Matron than for him. Like a good horse-trainer, she was totally unafraid of her charges, and unemotionally loving with them.

'I'll miss you,' said Laura. 'You will write and tell me how it goes, won't you? And what about the paper?'

'I'm taking unpaid leave. But they'll pay me for anything I send back that they can use.'

Larry and Judy, ringing from America, were horrified. 'You're not all alone, on Christmas Day? That's terrible.'

'We're enjoying it,' said Laura.

'What are you having for dinner?' Judy could not imagine the kitchen of the Grange without the smell of turkey at Christmas.

'Cold pheasant, not cooked by me. Bought. And lots of champagne.'

Over dinner John gave a toast: 'To the family.

Loved ones far away.'

'Oh, John, darling. I do worry about them all. I wish Mary would marry Luke. But it's Peter I worry about most. He's such a loving person. He needs a home and children. I know Fabiola's years younger than him, but I do wish . . .'

'My love, you've just got to leave it to him to sort his life out. They've all got to sort their lives out. We had to, after all.'

'But,' said Laura, 'they seem to have much more complicated lives than we had.'

'What do you mean, had? *Have*, if you don't mind.'

While Laura and John were enjoying their quiet Christmas, things were coming to a head at the Hotel Iris. Peter was aware that he had become far too fond of Fabiola. Sadly, he decided that the only honourable solution was to remove himself from the scene. Larry Cunningham was surprised by a sudden offer from his brother-in-law to come to Chicago and work for him. But with Judy now deeply and happily involved in his business, he really had no need of Peter. As tactfully as he could, he conveyed this fact.

So Peter hovered on, and Fabiola loved him more and more. At last seeing all too clearly what was happening to their beloved daughter, Maria and Giovanni persuaded her to go to college.

What happened in the end? Maria and Giovanni had reckoned without the sexuality that love for Peter had awakened in their virtuous girl. They might as well have saved themselves the trouble of getting her into college. In the second year, she began an affair with a fellow student. She was not in the least bit in love with him, but, confused and unhappy, she persuaded herself that she was, and married him. In an odd way, this worked out for the best. There was, eventually, to be a future together for her and Peter.

J. L. was destined to be an only child. However, he was an only child with two parents who had at last grown up. He did, of course, get very spoilt. But being somewhat like his Uncle Luke by nature, he remained sweet and sunny even at his naughtiest.

He got to know his Uncle Luke very well. He often visited, with pretty Mary, whom J. L. was forbidden to call Aunty. 'I am not your aunty, and even if I was I'm not going to be called aunty by a man who will be taller than me in a few years' time.' J. L., entranced at being called a man, rubbed his paw appreciatively over Mary's expensive silky tights.

'That,' said his Uncle Luke, 'will do. Keep your hands to yourself, my boy.'

Judy Cunningham's step-children soon found they had not only acquired a little half-sister, but very soon two half-brothers as well.

Pamela Bartlett bought herself an expensive and elaborate computer. Unfortunately it was unable to write a book, so it wound up as a plaything for Toby.

Laura and John Fenby settled down to grow old gracefully. John never learnt to cook, but he got better and better at shopping for treat foods. One day he plugged in the vacuum cleaner, but it blew up, so Mrs Bean confiscated it. It's a wise man, she told him, who knows the limitations of his abilities.

*Also by Fanny Frewen and available in Arrow*

## THE SUNLIGHT ON THE GARDEN

Laura and John Fenby have lived in Swanmere for thirty years. Surrounded by neighbours and with their children grown up, their place in the village is comfortable and secure, their daily lives ordered and rewarding.

Nearby live Marion and Jeremy Clark. Jeremy commutes to London where he visits his mistresses and lives a life unknown to his wife. Meanwhile Marion buries herself in the village and mourns the fact that she has never given Jeremy a child.

When the calm is broken with the news that Laura's poisonous and indomitable mother is to move in with them, Laura recognises that life will change. But what she cannot know is that it is her son Peter who will provoke the biggest upheavals of all. For as Peter, unhappy and directionless, turns to Marion for support, he provokes a chain of events that will transform all their lives.

*Also available in Arrow*

# MADENSKY SQUARE

## Eva Ibbotson

An enchanting tale of life and love in Imperial Vienna.

Susanna Weber is renowned for producing the most elegant, exquisite couture in Vienna. As all of fashionable society passes through her fitting room, Susanna touches numerous lives as matchmaker, comforter, confidante . . . and passionate lover.

From the impoverished yet proud Countess von Metz, to Nini the passionate Hungarian anarchist; from Sigismund Kraszinsky, the young musical prodigy, to Susanna's hidden lover himself, Eva Ibbotson conjures up a perfect miniature of a vanished society. But while the world hurtles towards war, the secrets and sorrows which lie behind Susanna's bewitching charm emerge as she and her friends live out the last, glittering days of Imperial Vienna in the idyllic surroundings of Madensky Square.

Praise for *Madensky Square*:

'Remarkable . . . in Susanna Weber, Eva Ibbotson has created a character worth caring about'
*The New York Times Book Review*

# A SONG FOR SUMMER

## Eva Ibbotson

When Ellen Carr, daughter of a militant suffragette and raised to be an intellectual, takes a job in Austria as housemother at the Hallendorf School of Music, Drama and the Dance she simply wants to cook beautiful food. What she finds when she reaches Schloss Hallendorf is an eccentrically magical world occupied by wild children, naked Harmony teachers, experimental dancers and a tortoise on wheels.

Life in Hallendorf seems idyllic, but outside the castle Hitler's Reich is already casting its menacing shadow over Europe and the persecutions have begun. Through her growing friendship with the mysterious groundsman Marek, Ellen encounters the dreadful reality of flight from Nazi Germany – and, on the brink of war, discovers a passion that will shape her life.

In this witty, touching and above all delightful novel, Eva Ibbotson combines an immensely satisfying love story with a gripping account of the gathering storm of war. *A Song for Summer* is a joy to read.

Praise for *A Song for Summer*:

'both romantic and entrancing . . . a quiet joy'
Nicola Beauman, *Hampstead & Highgate Express*

# OTHER TITLES AVAILABLE IN ARROW

| | | | |
|---|---|---|---|
| ☐ | The Sunlight on the Garden | Fanny Frewen | £5.99 |
| ☐ | Madensky Square | Eva Ibbotson | £5.99 |
| ☐ | A Song for Summer | Eva Ibbotson | £5.99 |
| ☐ | A Countess Below Stairs | Eva Ibbotson | £5.99 |
| ☐ | A Price for Everything | Mary Sheepshanks | £5.99 |
| ☐ | Facing the Music | Mary Sheepshanks | £5.99 |
| ☐ | Picking up the Pieces | Mary Sheepshanks | £5.99 |
| ☐ | Breaking the Chain | Maggie Makepeace | £5.99 |
| ☐ | Travelling Hopefully | Maggie Makepeace | £5.99 |
| ☐ | Night Shall Overtake Us | Kate Saunders | £6.99 |
| ☐ | Wild Young Bohemians | Kate Saunders | £5.99 |
| ☐ | Lily-Josephine | Kate Saunders | £5.99 |
| ☐ | The Anniversary | Ann Swinfen | £5.99 |
| ☐ | The Travellers | Ann Swinfen | £5.99 |
| ☐ | The Hours of the Night | Sue Gee | £5.99 |

ALL BOOKS ARE AVAILABLE THROUGH MAIL ORDER OR FROM YOUR LOCAL BOOKSHOP AND NEWSAGENT.

PLEASE SEND CHEQUE/EUROCHEQUE/POSTAL ORDER (STERLING ONLY) ACCESS, VISA, MASTERCARD, DINERS CARD, SWITCH OR AMEX.

| | | | | | | | | | | | | | | | |
|---|---|---|---|---|---|---|---|---|---|---|---|---|---|---|---|
| | | | | | | | | | | | | | | | |

EXPIRY DATE ................. SIGNATURE ............................................

PLEASE ALLOW 75 PENCE PER BOOK FOR POST AND PACKING U.K.

OVERSEAS CUSTOMERS PLEASE ALLOW £1.00 PER COPY FOR POST AND PACKING.

ALL ORDERS TO:

RANDOM HOUSE, BOOK SERVICE BY POST, TBS LIMITED, THE BOOK SERVICE, COLCHESTER ROAD, FRATING GREEN, COLCHESTER, ESSEX CO7 7DW.

NAME.............................................................................................

ADDRESS ....................................................................................

....................................................................................................

Please allow 28 days for delivery. Please tick box if you do not wish to receive any additional information ☐

Prices and availability subject to change without notice.